Usborne Illustrated

Ballet
Stories

Usborne Illustrated

Ballet Stories

Retold by
Susanna Davidson,
Katie Daynes, Megan Cullis
and Sarah Courtauld

Illustrated by
Yvonne Gilbert Nanos

Contents

The fairy tale of Cinderella has been told for
hundreds of years. In the 1940s, Sergei Prokofiev
composed an enchanting ballet score, based on a
17th-century version of the story by Charles Perrault.

Cinderella

A large, run-down town house was basking in the late summer sun. Once upon a time, laughter and singing would have floated through its rooms, but now the voices of two bossy sisters blasted from the windows. Today, they were arguing over an embroidered shawl.

"*I'm* wearing it to the ball!" shouted the younger, shorter sister.

"No, *I* am!" yelled the older, taller one.

They yanked at each end of the shawl, in a clumsy dance around the living room. Suddenly it ripped apart and both sisters fell with a THUMP onto the hard, oak floor.

As they squabbled over whose fault it was, their beautiful stepsister, Cinderella, sat downstairs in the kitchen, sewing silk bows for them. Cinderella didn't own any pretty clothes. She'd been invited to the prince's ball that evening, along with all the other girls in the land, but her horrible stepsisters wouldn't let her go.

"It's only for refined ladies like ourselves," they'd told her, "not for servants in tatty rags."

Cinderella sighed.

"I wish I could see the royal palace," she thought. She looked glumly at the pile of dirty dishes waiting for her by the sink, then at the little portrait of her mother on the mantelpiece. "Oh mother, if only you were still alive..."

Just then, she felt a large hand on her shoulder. She turned to see her father smiling awkwardly.

"I thought I'd find you here," he said. He loved his daughter dearly, but he wasn't brave enough to stand up to his ghastly stepdaughters. Picking up the portrait of his dead wife, his eyes filled with tears. "Life used to be so jolly," he said wistfully.

At that moment, the two ugly sisters burst in.

"Lazing around as usual, Cinderella?" they shrieked. "Leaving your poor sisters to dress for the ball on their own?"

"She's sewing your bows..." began Cinderella's father, timidly.

"Don't give her excuses," the taller sister snapped. "My toenails need trimming!"

"And my nose hairs need plucking," added the smaller sister.

DING-A-LING! Cinderella was saved from these gruesome tasks by the doorbell. An old woman stood hunched on the doorstep, leaning on a long white stick.

"Could you spare me a crumb to eat?" she asked.

Cinderella found a bread roll she'd been saving for her tea and handed it to the old woman.

"Don't give her anything!" cried the older sister, diving between them. She was about to say more, but a wave of the woman's stick forced her lips together. Another wave, and the old woman was gone.

DING-A-LING! Immediately, the doorbell rang again. It was

a dressmaker carrying extravagant new outfits for each of the ugly sisters.

DING-A-LING! A shoemaker entered with two pairs of pointy, high-heeled shoes.

DING-A-LING! Two feathered hats arrived in enormous boxes.

DING-A-LING! A hairdresser entered and tried to pin up the sisters' hair.

Giddy with excitement, the ugly sisters attempted to get ready. They squeezed themselves into corsets, streaked their faces with lipstick and eyeliner, and pinned elaborate wigs over their hair.

DING-A-LING! It was a dance teacher, come to give the ugly sisters a lesson. Cinderella and her father watched as he began.

"Copy me," said the teacher, stepping forward gracefully and gesturing to his pupils to follow.

Heads held high, the ugly sisters stumbled

flat-footed across the room after him.

"Try again," said the teacher calmly.

As they tried, the shorter sister managed to trip over her dress. The teacher took her hand to steady her. That made the taller sister jealous, so she tripped over on purpose to get the teacher's attention! The teacher decided to end the lesson there, and politely excused himself.

DING-A-LING! A coach had arrived to take them to the ball.

"Don't we look divine," cooed the sisters.

Cinderella thought it best not to answer. She walked her father to the door and the ugly sisters whisked him away.

"At least now I'll have some peace and quiet," sighed Cinderella. She picked up a broom – but instead of sweeping, she imagined she was at the ball and that the broom was the prince. Her dainty feet twirled around the empty kitchen...

A sudden flourish of music made her freeze. Out of nowhere, the old woman with the white stick had reappeared.

"Oh, um, are you still hungry?" asked Cinderella, flustered. "I don't know if there's any bread left..."

"I'm not here for bread, I'm here for YOU!" announced the old woman. With a dramatic swirl, she threw off her cloak to reveal a dazzling fairy dress and wings. "I'm your fairy godmother and I'm not going to let you miss the prince's ball. What we need is a touch of magic..."

Cinderella stared in amazement as the fairy waved her stick – which was really a wand. The kitchen, usually so dreary, now sparkled with fairy dust. Pots and pans faded away and the room was filled with a magical light. A fairy for each season appeared and danced before Cinderella.

She watched, spellbound, as the freshness of spring blossomed into bright summer petals, and a gust of russet leaves gave way to glistening winter.

"Now bring me the biggest pumpkin from your garden," ordered the fairy godmother.

Cinderella placed the heavy pumpkin on the floor and the fairies of the seasons made a circle around it. In a sudden flash, the pumpkin was transformed into a golden coach, pulled by a pair of fine white horses.

A footman invited Cinderella to climb on board. She lifted her foot onto the step – and gasped. On her feet were sparkling glass slippers, and her tatty rags were now an elegant satin ball gown!

"Enjoy yourself," called her godmother, as the coach pulled away. "But make sure you leave the ball by midnight, before the magic wears off."

At the prince's palace, the ball had already begun. Stately tunes from the orchestra filled the air, while guests arrived and admired the lavish ballroom.

The court jester amused everyone with songs and jokes, then led them all in a formal dance.

When the ugly sisters arrived, the other guests turned and stared.

"Do you think they've escaped from the zoo?" the jester whispered, making a group of ladies titter behind their fans.

The sisters didn't even notice, but marched confidently onto the dance floor.

"I'm going to dance with that one," said the younger sister, pointing at a tall man in uniform.

"No you're not, he's mine," decided the older sister. She flounced up to the unfortunate man and seized his hand.

He was very well mannered and didn't once complain, even though she danced like a baboon and trampled on his toes three times. Finally, he was rescued by a trumpet fanfare, announcing the arrival of the prince.

Dressed in a dashing outfit, the handsome prince made his way down the grand staircase. The ladies in the room gazed up at him, fluttering their fans and trying to catch his attention. The ugly sisters elbowed their way to the front, each hoping to be the prince's first dance partner.

Then another blast from the trumpets announced a late arrival. Everyone turned to see who dared to arrive after the prince.

Framed in the doorway and glowing against the night sky stood Cinderella in her magical gown. At the sight of so many staring faces, she was tempted to turn and flee.

Instead, she took a deep breath, steadied her nerves and slowly descended the stairs.

The prince watched Cinderella in wonder. Without saying a word, he offered her his hand and guided her onto the dance floor. Then they began to glide around the room, as if they had been dancing together all their lives.

"She's so graceful," whispered one of the guests.

"She must be a princess," added another.

On the edge of the dance floor, the ugly sisters stood scowling.

"Who does she think she is, just waltzing in like that?" they muttered. Never in their wildest dreams did they realize they were talking about their own stepsister.

When the dance came to an end, the prince called for refreshments. His servants brought a silver serving dish piled high with oranges, the most exotic fruit in his kingdom. He presented one to Cinderella, then he took pity on the ugly sisters and gave them each an orange too. While they bickered over whose was the biggest, the prince and Cinderella tiptoed away.

The next dance tune began and the ugly sisters gazed grumpily across the ballroom. When it became clear that no one was going to ask them to dance, they linked arms with each other and trotted clumsily across the ballroom.

Meanwhile, Cinderella and the prince were lost in a dream. They danced out onto the moonlit terrace, through the palace gardens and back into the ballroom.

Cinderella wished the evening would last forever – but all too soon she heard bells chiming midnight and remembered her godmother's warning.

"I'm so sorry, I must go," she whispered.

"Please don't," said the prince.

But Cinderella slipped from his grasp and ran for the door, weaving her way through the other dancing guests. She fled the palace without a second to spare. Her dress had turned back to rags and one of her shoes was missing.

The poor prince rushed after her, but she was already lost from view. All that was left of his enchanting princess was a dainty glass slipper.

Cinderella's heart was pounding as she slipped in through the back door and down to the cold, dark kitchen. She stirred the dying embers of the fire and added some more coal. Had the whole evening been a dream? She looked down in dismay at her tattered rags, then spied a glimmer of gold. She was still wearing one of the slippers!

Holding the slipper in one hand, Cinderella moved it gracefully through the air, reliving her dance with the prince.

The SLAM of the front door brought her back to the present and she hastily hid the slipper.

"Oh, my poor feet," moaned the elder stepsister, clumping into the room.

"Undo my corset before it kills me!" cried the younger one.

Cinderella fussed around the ugly sisters, unlacing their dresses, while they talked about the ball and lied about all the men they'd danced with.

"Look what the prince gave me," boasted the eldest, holding up an orange.

"And me!" added the younger one.

Behind them, Cinderella's father slumped down in a chair. He'd found the whole event exhausting. But the evening wasn't over yet...

A sudden blast of trumpets made everyone jump. The door swung open and in walked four courtiers, the jester and the prince himself!

There was purpose in the prince's stride and a gilded glass slipper in his hand.

"I intend to marry the girl whose foot fits this slipper," he announced, "and I will travel the entire kingdom until I find her."

"Travel no further," cried the older sister, wrenching off her shoe. "It's me!"

She snatched the slipper from the prince and tried to ram it onto her foot.

The slipper barely covered her toes.

"Let me try!" cried the other sister. But no amount of squeezing and tugging could make the slipper fit.

"Is there anyone else here who could try it?" asked the prince.

Before Cinderella's father could speak, the ugly sisters shouted, "Of course not! Only us."

Cinderella stepped back into the shadows, praying that the prince wouldn't see her. She wanted him to remember her as a beautiful princess, not a ragged-looking kitchen maid. But as she moved, her slipper fell from its hiding place to the ground and twinkled in the firelight.

The prince saw it at once and rushed forward with his slipper. They matched! Looking up in excitement, he saw Cinderella in the shadows.

"Please try on this slipper," he asked her gently.

The jester brought forward a stool and everyone else gathered around to watch. Timidly, Cinderella sat down, not daring to look at the prince. Kneeling before her, the prince easily slid the slipper onto her slender foot.

"The princess from the ball!" he cried.

"But I'm not a princess, I'm only a poor girl in rags," said Cinderella with a sigh.

"Then marry me and become MY princess!" implored the prince.

Cinderella finally dared to look up at him. He took her in his arms and they started moving together, dancing as they had done at the ball.

The stepsisters looked on, horrified. Was their shabby stepsister really the girl from the ball? Did that mean the girl they'd been bullying for years was about to become royalty? They hurriedly began curtseying and cooing.

"We always knew you were special."

"Please forgive us, dearest sister..."

Cinderella laughed. She couldn't hold a grudge on a day like today. Happiness filled her heart.

"I forgive you," she said, kindly.

As she spoke, a magical glow filled the room. The fairy godmother glided in, her smile reaching from cheek to cheek. With a flurry of wings, the other fairies arrived too. Then the dark kitchen disappeared and everyone was transported to the palace gardens.

Dressed once more in her beautiful gown, Cinderella gazed up at her handsome prince.

"Promise you won't leave me this time," he said.

"I promise!" Cinderella replied, happily.

A tragic love story about a prince and the Queen
of the Swans, this ballet was first performed in 1877.
It was inspired by German and Russian folk tales,
with music by Russian composer, Pyotr Tchaikovsky.

Swan Lake

As the sun slowly sank in an apricot sky, the royal castle hummed with excitement. It was Prince Siegfried's twenty-first birthday and the celebrations were about to begin. Maids and footmen rushed around the cobbled courtyard, adding finishing touches to the tables and decorations. They lit lanterns, carried great jugs of wine to the long trestle tables and, last of all, heaved open the castle gates.

Villagers flooded into the courtyard and gazed around themselves in delight. At the front of the group stood a small girl, open-mouthed. She tugged at her mother's hand.

"It's like fairyland!" she whispered.

A sudden fanfare made everyone jump.

"Make way, make way," cried a royal courtier. "Prince Siegfried is coming!"

A tall, handsome figure strode out through the castle arch. He beamed at the crowd of expectant faces and raised his hand in welcome.

"Happy birthday, Your Highness," chorused the villagers, raising their goblets.

"Thank you, my loyal friends," replied the prince. "Now let the dancing begin!"

The orchestra struck up a waltz and a few brave people began to dance. Before long, the whole

courtyard was alive with music and movement. Couples twirled across the cobbles as the swell of violins filled the air.

Prince Siegfried looked on with a happy smile. When he turned to speak to his friends, he was surprised by Benno's anxious face.

"What's wrong?" asked the prince.

"The queen," whispered Benno. "She's heading this way."

The queen's arrival sent an icy chill through the festivities. Musicians stopped playing and dancers froze, but the queen didn't seem to mind. She made her way through the crowd, heading straight for her son, her head held high and her stride long and purposeful.

"Happy birthday, my dear son," she said, planting a cold kiss on Siegfried's cheek.

"Here is my present for you." She beckoned to one of her servants, who presented Siegfried with a silver crossbow.

The young prince gasped. "Thank you, Mother," he began. "It's wonderful..."

But the queen held up a hand to silence him. "Now you are twenty-one, it's time you grew up and got married." She spoke firmly, without warmth. "I have invited the most beautiful ladies in the kingdom to your birthday ball tomorrow night – and I want you to choose one of them as your wife."

Prince Siegfried bowed politely. "If that is your wish," he said through clenched teeth.

Her gift and message delivered, the queen swept up her skirts and swiftly left.

With a tap of his baton, the conductor restarted the orchestra. Soon the courtyard was a whirl once more, as if nothing had changed... except for the prince, who now sat forlornly in the shadows.

"Cheer up," said Benno, laying a hand on his friend's shoulder.

Siegfried let out a heavy sigh. "I can't just pick a wife like *that*," he said, snapping his fingers. "Besides, I'm too young to get married. And I only want to marry someone I love..."

Benno saw the lantern flame glinting on Siegfried's new crossbow and an idea came to him. "I know what will cheer you up. Hunting!"

At that moment, a flock of swans flew overhead, their arched bodies silhouetted in the twilight sky.

Siegfried spied the birds and his smile returned. "Quick, after those swans!" he cried, jumping to his feet and snatching up his crossbow.

Benno beckoned for their friends to follow and they all set out to follow the flock.

"This way!" called Siegfried.

As the swans flew over the royal forest, the young men were in hot pursuit. They wove their way among the trees until they reached the shores of a wide lake.

"Go on ahead," Siegfried whispered, gesturing to the others. "I'll hide here."

Crouched low among the reeds, Siegfried looked out across the still water, gleaming in the silvery moonlight.

He watched and waited, his crossbow ready at his side. Then he spied the swans gliding silently across the lake's surface. With a steady hand, he drew back his crossbow and took aim.

"Just a little closer," he murmured.

Before he could release his arrow, there was a flurry of beating wings and a figure emerged – no longer a wild swan but a beautiful woman.

Siegfried gazed in wonder as she shook the water from her downy white dress and stepped gracefully out of the lake. Her face was as pale as porcelain and on her head sat a feathered crown.

"Who are you?" Siegfried blurted out.

The woman drew back in terror.

"I'm sorry," said Siegfried, speaking more softly this time and lowering his crossbow. "I won't hurt you, I promise."

The swan woman looked warily at the prince, as if deciding whether to trust him. "I am Odette," she said finally. "Queen of the Swans."

She gestured to the swans who had landed behind her. One by one they were emerging from the water, transforming before Siegfried's eyes from swans to women. They arched their necks gracefully and smoothed their white dresses, as if preening their feathers. Siegfried stood mesmerized by the sight.

"We are under a spell to be swans by day," Odette explained. "Only between midnight and dawn can we become human again."

Siegfried stepped closer, keeping his movements slow and gentle so as not to alarm the swan queen.

He was filled with curiosity and sadness. "Who did this?" he asked her.

Odette replied with a single word: "Rothbart." The prince watched the swan princesses shiver and cower at the name. "He's the worst kind of magician," Odette went on, bowing her head with sorrow. "He's blacker than the night and more cunning than a fox. He watches over us in the form of an owl and has doomed us to be swans forever."

"Can't the spell be broken?" urged Siegfried. "There must be some way I can help you."

Odette shook her head. "The spell would only be broken if someone promised to marry me. They would have to swear to love me forever and never betray me."

At these words, Siegfried fell to his knees and took Odette's small hand in his. Engulfed by emotion, he barely thought of what he was saying.

"I promise to marry you!" he cried. "I will love you forever."

Siegfried's words rang out through the forest and echoed across the lake. The swan-maidens and Odette gazed at him, not daring to believe the spell could truly be broken.

"I will save you from Rothbart, Odette," Siegfried promised. He stood up and wrapped his arms protectively around her, feeling a profound love that he'd never experienced before.

Odette looked into his eyes and dared to hope.

Unknown to the young couple, the evil magician Rothbart had been watching all along from the shadows. Now he prowled back and forth, beating his dark wings in fury.

"That prince can't break my spell," he muttered. "I won't let him..." His scowl began to lift into a sneering smile. "I'll trick him, that's what I'll do. I'll make him betray Odette – then she will be under my power forever more!"

At first light, Rothbart rose high above the swan-maidens on his great black wings. "Go back to the lake!" he shouted.

Siegfried clung tightly to Odette. "No!" he cried. "I won't let him take you."

But Rothbart's magic was too powerful. It dragged Odette from Siegfried's arms. Already her human form was fading fast and soon Siegfried was standing helplessly alone by the lake. A deep cackle filled the air and a flock of swans soared across the dawn sky.

The following evening was the prince's birthday ball. The castle was crammed with guests and entertainers, who had journeyed from as far as Spain, Hungary, Poland and Italy. The great hall glowed with fiery candles and the air was thick with perfume.

The queen sat on a purple throne and studied her son's every move. He was dutifully dancing with all the ladies she'd invited, but it was plain to see that he didn't care for any of them. He barely looked at the pretty young lady he was dancing with now – and her father was the Archduke!

When the dance ended, Siegfried led her back to her seat, bowed curtly and turned away. The same thing happened in each of the following dances, until the music finally came to an end.

Then the queen rose from her throne and strode up to the prince. "So, my son," she said firmly, for all to hear, "which of these beautiful princesses are you going to take as your wife?"

There was a hushed silence around the room and Siegfried's reply rang out loud and clear.

"I cannot marry any of them," he declared.

The ladies he'd danced with blushed with embarrassment and the queen flushed with fury. Before she could find the words to reply, there was a loud thunderclap and the door to the great hall was flung open.

Framed in the entranceway stood two figures, a tall man dressed in the rich clothes of a count and a slender young woman. The count had thick black hair that rose up in feather-like tufts around his head, and there was something sinister about his sneering smile.

But Siegfried hardly noticed the count. His eyes were drawn instead to the mysterious young woman. She too was dressed in black and on her head she wore a silver crown, but it was her

porcelain face that made the prince rush forward.

"Odette?" he cried.

She did not reply, but he was sure it was her.

As the music began again, Siegfried invited the woman to dance and together they whirled across the room. Bewitched by his partner's beauty, Siegfried forgot about his mother, the other guests, the great hall... He could only stare into her glittering eyes.

The prince never heard the sound of fluttering wings at the window. He never noticed the white shadow in the moonlight, gazing at him mournfully and pleading for him to stop.

At the end of the dance, Siegfried turned to the astonished guests. "Meet my future wife," he announced, proudly holding up his dance partner's hand. "We will marry as soon as possible."

"Are you sure that you love her?" asked the count. "Do you swear it?"

"I swear it," answered Siegfried firmly.

There was a harsh cackle of laughter as the count flung off his robes. Siegfried stumbled back and gasped in horror. It was Rothbart!

"You have betrayed Odette," cried the evil magician. "The woman you have just sworn you love is, in fact, my daughter, Odile." He swept his cloak over Odile and, with another thunderclap, they vanished.

"I've been tricked!" moaned Siegfried. He looked around at the shocked faces at the ball and tore from the room without another word.

Siegfried sped as fast as he could to the lake, his feet barely touching the ground. He found the swan princesses huddled around Odette, trying to comfort her. He threw himself at Odette's feet.

"Forgive me," he begged. "I was tricked by Rothbart, but I never stopped loving you."

Odette looked up, tears glistening on her cheeks. She had wept as she'd watched Siegfried dance with Odile, and she had wept again when she had realized Rothbart's spell would never be broken. But now she was calm, soothed by Siegfried's presence.

"I knew Rothbart would try to stop us," she said. "I came to the castle to warn you, but I couldn't get in. I watched you from the window and saw you dancing with that woman. You looked so in love, but I felt sure she was evil."

"It was Odile, Rothbart's daughter," Siegfried explained. "He used his magic to make her look like you. Please forgive me."

"I do," Odette replied, and embraced him.

"We'll never be apart again," Siegfried promised.

"Too late!" roared a voice from the darkness.

Siegfried and Odette looked up in terror as Rothbart swept over them.

"Odette is mine," he snarled, snatching her away from the prince.

Siegfried turned to fight him, trying against all odds to rescue Odette from Rothbart's power.

As they fought, Odette managed to slip away.

"My darling prince," she called. "If I can't be with you, I'd rather die than be under Rothbart's spell." And with those words, she climbed up onto the rocks.

Rothbart and Siegfried turned in alarm to see Odette launch herself from the rocks and dive deep into the lake.

Swan Lake

There was hardly a ripple as the dark waters closed over her.

"Nooooo!" howled Rothbart, briefly loosening his grip on Siegfried.

The prince seized his moment and raced after Odette. "I can't lose you a second time!" he cried, throwing himself into the lake after her.

Rothbart let out another howl and sank down by the water's edge. United in death, the power of Odette and Siegfried's love was far greater than any of Rothbart's magic. With a hideous shriek, he collapsed to the ground. Nothing was left of him except a scattered heap of black feathers.

Moments later, the swan princesses crept out of hiding. They stood motionless, their faces wet

with tears. But, as the sun slowly rose in the morning sky, they gazed in wonder at their hands and feet. It was day, and they were still women. Rothbart's spell had finally been broken.

Based on a much-loved fairy tale, the ballet of
Sleeping Beauty was first performed in 1890.
The composer, Pyotr Tchaikovsky, took just
40 days to write the music.

Sleeping Beauty

*L*ong ago, in a fairytale castle far away, a kind-hearted queen gave birth to a rosy-cheeked daughter.

"This is the happiest day of my life!" declared the king. "What shall we call our bundle of joy?"

"How about Aurora," suggested the queen.

The king instantly agreed. "And we'll invite all the fairies in the kingdom to her christening," he announced.

The day of the christening dawned sunny and bright. A graceful fairy dressed in lilac danced into the castle to greet the royal parents. Six more fairies followed, wearing shimmering summer dresses.

"Your Majesties," said the Lilac Fairy with a dainty curtsey. "Please allow us to present your daughter with our gifts."

"With pleasure," replied the king and queen.

The Lilac Fairy stood back and gestured to the others. One by one, they twirled up to baby Aurora, who was sleeping soundly in her cradle.

"I give you beauty," said the first, with a flourish of her wand.

"A sweet temper," said the second.

"And grace," added the third.

"May you move like a ballerina," continued the fourth.

"Sing like a nightingale," chimed the fifth.

"And play all the instruments of the orchestra perfectly," said the sixth.

Before the Lilac Fairy could add her gift, there was a crash of thunder and a black cloud blotted out the sun. From the darkness swept another fairy – the wicked Carabosse – with her ugly rat servants prancing around her.

"Where was *my* invitation?" she spat, pointing a crooked finger at the king. "You have insulted me. Now it's my turn to give your daughter a gift."

"We're s-so s-sorry," stammered the king.

"There must have been some mistake," added the queen hastily.

But Carabosse had turned her piercing gaze on tiny Aurora. "I can't take away your beauty, my dear, but I can take away... your life." Sharp gasps filled the room, as Carabosse continued her evil curse. "One day, something sharp will prick your finger and you will fall down DEAD!" Then she let out a gruesome cackle that made the other fairies cower.

"Please don't do this, I beg you!" pleaded the queen. "She's only a baby."

But the queen's pleas only made Carabosse's cackles grow louder.

"Enough!" cried the Lilac Fairy, striding bravely forward and silencing Carabosse with a wave of her wand. "Do not despair," she told the king and queen. "I haven't offered your daughter my gift yet.

Although I can't break Carabosse's curse, I can weaken it. Aurora will prick her finger and fall, but she *won't* die. Instead, she will slip into a deep sleep until she is woken by a handsome prince."

The Lilac Fairy's kind words infuriated Carabosse. She swept her cloak around her and stormed out of the castle.

Slowly, the sun crept out from behind the cloud and spread light on the castle once more.

The years went by and Princess Aurora grew prettier each day. The king and queen loved to watch their cheerful daughter dance and sing, but Carabosse's curse still hung over them. All sharp objects were banished from the castle, every rose bush was cut down for fear of thorns, and the princess was never left alone.

For Aurora's sixteenth birthday, the king arranged a magnificent party. Sunshine flooded the royal gardens, guests met and mingled in the dappled shade and music floated on the warm summer air.

"Aurora," called the king, a twinkle in his eye. "Four birthday surprises have just arrived!"

The princess laughed to see four nervous princes standing behind her father.

Tales of her beauty had reached their distant kingdoms and now they all wanted to marry her.

The princes took turns dancing with Aurora. Charmed by her smile and beauty, they each offered their love and fortunes. Aurora thanked them graciously, but she didn't want a husband – she just wanted to dance.

Twirling away from her fourth suitor, the princess bumped into a wrinkled old lady.

"Oh, I'm so sorry," said Aurora, blushing.

"Don't worry, my dear," croaked the woman. "Look, I've brought you some flowers for your birthday today."

"Thank you, how kind," said the princess, taking the bouquet and admiring the fragrant but unfamiliar roses.

Immediately, three

concerned courtiers swooped to grab the flowers. Aurora thought it was a game and danced away across the lawn, waving the flowers above her head. As she tightened her grip, she felt a sharp prick.

"Ow!" she cried, dropping the bouquet and looking at her hand. A little drop of blood was forming on her fingertip. Her dance turned into a sway and the world started spinning. The faces around her blurred and merged together... then everything went blank.

The guests stared in horror as the princess fell to the ground. A familiar cackle filled the air and the old woman threw back her hood. It was Carabosse. After a gleeful look at the fallen princess, the evil fairy fled the castle grounds.

"My darling daughter!" wailed the queen, rushing to Aurora's side. She lifted her daughter's lifeless arm and let out a moan.

A swirl of purple announced the Lilac Fairy. "Remember, she's not dead, only sleeping," the fairy said softly. "Take her into the castle and lay her on her bed." Four servants carried the princess inside and the party guests followed in a hushed procession.

Left alone in the garden, the Lilac Fairy watched as creeping vines swiftly covered the castle walls. In no time, the building was overgrown and everyone inside was slumbering peacefully.

One hundred years later, only a few miles from Aurora's palace, a royal hunt was taking place in a forest. While half the riders galloped off after

a deer, the others stopped to rest their horses in
a quiet clearing.

"Let's dance!" suggested one of the pretty ladies.

The men were all keen – except for young Prince
Florimund. He forced himself to smile and bow to
his dance partner, but he really wasn't in the mood.

"Another dance!" cried a lord, when it was over.

"Not now," replied the prince. "You'd better catch
up with the hunt before you lose them."

"Aren't you coming too?" said the lord.

"I'll be along soon," he promised.

As the guests left the leafy glade, Florimund
let out a deep sigh. He felt trapped in his role as
prince. Hunts and balls were all very well, but he
longed for something more meaningful. As he
sighed again, a fairy dressed in lilac appeared.

"You look sad," she said. "Let me show you
something to lift your spirits."

She swept her wand through the air and a wonderful vision appeared before them...

There stood Princess Aurora, surrounded by fairies in glittering dresses. Her grace and beauty made Florimund want to reach out and touch her. He took a step forward, but the fairies blocked his path. He moved left, then right, trying to dodge past them, his eyes never leaving the princess's face. Finally he was close enough to embrace her, but in that instant she was gone.

The lovestruck prince turned to the Lilac Fairy.

"Who was that?" he asked. "Where has she gone? I've never seen anyone so wonderful in my life. I must find her!"

"Then follow me," said the fairy.

From the glade, the fairy guided Florimund through the forest. His step was quick but she was quicker, dancing over logs and streams. At last,

they reached a shimmering lake and boarded a
fairy boat. As they glided over silver water, the
fairy pointed to a distant tower.

"The princess is sleeping in there," she said.

Florimund felt his heart beat faster. "Then I will
go and wake her," he replied.

The castle entrance was barely visible under a
century of creeping vines and cobwebs. Prince
Florimund strode up to the rusted gates and
boldly pushed them apart.

Fighting his way through the overgrown garden,
he eventually reached the castle steps. When he
creaked open the oak doors, he saw two footmen
sprawled on the floor. Their loud snores told him
they were soundly asleep.

Then the Lilac Fairy stepped forward, her
shining wand casting light down the dark corridor.

"This way," she whispered.

She led the prince through the silent castle, up a forgotten spiral staircase and into the princess's room. Aurora lay on a four-poster bed, as pale as her silk pillow and perfectly still.

"But she's dead!" exclaimed the prince.

"No, only sleeping," said the fairy, "and waiting for you to wake her."

The prince didn't know who the princess was, or why she was asleep in a castle lost in time. All he knew was that she was the most wonderful person he had ever seen. He took her small hand in his. Slowly, Aurora's eyes fluttered open. Florimund stood back shyly, but Aurora looked up at him and smiled.

"Thank you for waking me," she whispered.

The delighted prince helped Aurora to her feet and led her down the stairs. He was so dazzled by her beauty, he didn't notice the castle changing

around him. The vines and cobwebs melted away, while all over the castle, people were waking and stretching after their long sleep.

"Come and meet my parents," said Aurora.

She whisked him into the main hall, where her parents were dusting their robes and straightening their crowns.

"Aurora!" cried the king and queen together.

"Meet the prince who broke Carabosse's spell!" replied the princess. She turned to smile at her rescuer, only to find him kneeling on the floor.

"Aurora," he said, "will you marry me?"

"I'd love to," said Aurora, beaming.

Aurora and Florimund's wedding day was a joyful whirl of celebration. The castle was decorated from tower to cellar, and delicious smells wafted from the bustling kitchen. By noon, a stream of family and friends was entering the grand hall.

Delightful characters from other fairy tales came to entertain the happy couple. First, Puss in Boots leaped and pranced across the dance floor with a dainty white cat. Then Little Red Riding Hood appeared, holding a basket of food. Behind her crept the big, bad wolf. He chased Red Riding Hood around the room in a playful dance, before carrying her off over his shoulder.

The guests had barely taken a breath when Cinderella danced into the room, searching for Prince Charming. He followed soon after, holding out the golden slipper she'd lost and together they twirled elegantly around the dance floor.

Once the entertainment was over, all eyes turned to Aurora and Florimund. Filled with love for each other, they began a dreamlike dance. Hovering overhead, the Lilac Fairy held high her wand and rejoiced in the happy scene.

This ballet is based on a Spanish novel by
Miguel de Cervantes. The best-known version was
first performed by Russia's Bolshoi Ballet in 1869.

Don Quixote

"He's crazy! All he does is read stories about knights..."

"He even thinks he is one!"

Don Quixote's servants dropped their voices to a whisper as the old man shuffled into the room, his eyes fixed on the book in his hand.

Don Quixote was so absorbed in his book, he didn't even notice his servants huddled in the corner, nor his old friend, Carrasco, who had come to see if the stories were true – if Don Quixote really was losing his mind.

Oblivious to all, Don Quixote sat down in his chair, put down his book, closed his eyes and began to dream... *he was jousting in a foreign field, wrestling with giants, rescuing damsels in distress. And not just any damsel – he was rescuing his adored... his beautiful Dulcinea; a lady so lovely she must be a goddess...*

He was woken by the sound of shattering glass as his servant, Sancho Panza, came leaping in through the window, pursued by a hoard of screaming women.

"That fat man stole my goose!" shrieked one,

trying to swipe him with a cloth.

"And my bread!" screeched another, hitting Sancho Panza on the head with a wooden spoon.

"He came sneaking into the market like a common thief," added a third. "I tell you, he should be punished."

"Yes, yes, and so he will be," said Don Quixote, ready to say anything to be rid of these shouting women who had disturbed his dreams. "Now away with you! All of you! Leave my house."

With relief, he watched the women leave, and his house settle back into peace and quiet once more. Then he turned to his servant.

"Sancho Panza," he declared. "I have decided to set out in search of adventure. I am a knight and it is my duty to defend the virtue of maidens, to fight dragons and giants. You are to be my squire. Now, where's my helmet..."

To Sancho Panza's surprise, one of the other servants reached for an empty shaving basin and plonked it on Don Quixote's head.

"Ah! Perfect!" said Don Quixote. "And now for my lance," he added, picking up a heavy iron poker. "Now, pass me the rest of my outfit."

Sancho Panza cast his eyes around the study, then pulled down a battered sword, shield and spear, hanging on the wall.

"Are you ready?" asked Don Quixote.

"I'm ready," replied Sancho Panza, with a resigned shrug. What else could he do, after all, but follow his crazy master? Don Quixote leaped on his horse, Rosinante, and off they rode together on their adventure...

"Aha!" said Don Quixote as, after many hours, they reached a town square. "I wonder what we will find here, Sancho Panza."

There was a large crowd gathered in front of an inn, cheering excitedly. A group of street dancers, dressed in flaming red cloaks, were putting on a show. They sprang this way and that, flourishing their cloaks, enacting a dramatic bull fight. Local girls danced with fans, red flowers tucked into their hair. They stepped and twirled to the jangle of tambourines and the click of castanets.

Then the crowds parted and just two dancers were left – a man and a woman. They were Kitri, the innkeeper's daughter, and Basilio, the man she loved. He handed her a flower, serenaded her with his guitar and together they swept across the cobblestones, until a cry came from the inn.

"Away with you!" the innkeeper shouted at Basilio. "Don't come near my daughter. You're nothing but a barber. You're not good enough for her. She is going to marry Gamache, a nobleman."

"Please Father," begged Kitri. "Let me marry Basilio, I beg of you."

"Never," replied her father.

No sooner had the innkeeper pushed Basilio away, than Gamache flounced into the town square. He wore a long silken cloak and a feather in his hat. The innkeeper summoned his daughter, but Kitri was having none of it.

"Basilio is the one I love," she told her father. She looked at the simpering Gamache and laughed. "I'll never marry him!" Then she turned on her heel and strode away.

"Oh!" gasped Don Quixote, as one wakening from a dream. He clutched Sancho Panza's arm and pointed to Kitri's retreating back. "That must be Dulcinea, the lady of my heart. I will talk to her father and ask for permission to introduce myself."

Don Quixote bowed low before the innkeeper. "This must be your castle, my lord," he said, pointing to the inn. "I would like to pay my respects to your beautiful daughter."

The innkeeper puffed himself out with pride. "My castle, you say? Well, of course, of course. But first come inside and I'll show you around." And he gestured to Gamache to follow them.

Sancho Panza shook his head and stayed in the town square, where a group of young people crowded around him. They began to tease him and laugh at him. They spun him around and tossed him up into the air...

"Stop that!" shouted Don Quixote, rushing back outside to save his squire, the innkeeper following on behind.

"Where is my daughter?" demanded the

innkeeper. "I thought she was out here, with you."

Everyone in the square shook their heads. "We haven't seen her," they cried.

"She has gone!" declared Gamache, searching the crowds. "And so has Basilio."

"Let's find them!" said the innkeeper. "And then I will announce her marriage to you, Gamache."

"And we will go too!" whispered Don Quixote. "Come, squire. This will be our next adventure..."

Don Quixote and Sancho Panza rode out of town until they reached a gypsy camp in the foothills. Word had already spread of the old man on a quest to nowhere, who thought he lived in a fantasy land of giants and monsters and damsels in distress.

As soon as they saw him coming, the gypsy chief decided to put on a show in order to have some fun at the old man's expense. So he donned a crown and sat as if on a throne. When Don Quixote saw him, he promptly dropped to his knees to pay homage.

"Your Majesty," cried Don Quixote.

"Welcome," said the gypsy chief, hiding his smiles. "Your fame goes before you, brave knight. We are putting on a festival just for you. Come, sit beside me."

"With pleasure," replied Don Quixote. He sat down beside the chief, just as the gypsies began to dance.

"And now for the puppet show," announced the gypsy chief.

All went well until Don Quixote confused the puppet girl for Dulcinea. He leaped from his seat, clutching his spear. "My lady love!" he declared. Then he pointed at the other puppets. "She is being attacked. I must save her."

"Run!" said the gypsies in panic, as they saw Don Quixote coming towards them, waving his spear. They promptly dropped the puppet strings and fled into the woods.

Don Quixote stopped in his tracks as the puppets collapsed around him, falling to the ground in crumpled heaps. "I've won!" he exclaimed to Sancho Panza. "Victory is mine. Our work here is done, my squire!"

He called to his horse and began to ride for the hills, poor Sancho Panza still following on behind.

On the hill tops stood several large windmills, standing out against the sky, their sails like waving arms. Don Quixote stopped and stared at them for a moment, then began waving his spear about in excitement. "Giants!" he shouted, pointing to the windmills. "We must attack!"

"Come back!" called Sancho Panza.

But there was no stopping his master, who rushed at the nearest windmill, once more wildly waving his spear.

Don Quixote galloped closer and closer, fearless in his speed and war-like cries.

Sancho Panza could only watch in horror as the windmill's sails swooped down and caught Don Quixote by his cloak, flinging him up, up, up into the air, then hurling him back to the ground.

Sancho Panza ran to his master, but Don Quixote lay deeply asleep and nothing would wake him. He was dreaming again...

In this dream he carried a shining sword. One by one, monsters approached him with gnashing teeth and gleaming horns, lashing tails and razor claws.

Don Quixote smote them with his sword, but even as they were defeated, there came a giant spider, spinning a dreadful, sticky, thickly-knotted web.

Courageous to the last, Don Quixote slashed at the spider, slicing it in two. Then he gasped. The web had vanished and in its place was a beautiful garden, filled with women. Among them was Dulcinea, the lady of his heart. In the next moment, to his dismay, the dream vanished...

He woke to find himself at an inn. Kitri and Basilio were standing over him, greeting him like an old friend. "Sancho Panza brought you here to rest," said Kitri.

But before she could say more, her father and Gamache stormed into the inn.

"There is to be no more running away!" yelled her father. "You WILL marry Gamache."

"I can't bear it!" sobbed Basilio. He took out a sword and thrust it into his chest.

With a wail, the broken-hearted Kitri flung herself across his fallen body.

"A tragedy!" said Don Quixote. "You, innkeeper, should have listened to your daughter's heart."

"Give Basilio his dying wish," pleaded Kitri.

"Yes," insisted Don Quixote. "Give this young couple your blessing. Basilio is sure to die. Why not ease his last moments?"

The innkeeper looked at their earnest faces. "Fine, fine!" he snapped. "What does it matter now! You have my blessing to marry Basilio."

At those words Basilio leaped to his feet, kissing the innkeeper and shouting for joy.

"You're not hurt at all!" cried the innkeeper. "I've been tricked."

"We are to be married!" said Kitri smiling, her hand in Basilio's. She turned to Don Quixote. "And you will be our most important guest."

The wedding feast was soon prepared. There was merrymaking and dancing. Don Quixote watched it all with a benevolent smile.

"Thank you, great knight," called out Kitri. "And thanks to your faithful sword-bearer. This dance is for you."

As Kitri and Basilio whirled across the floor, the crowd cheered.

At the dance's end, an unfamiliar knight came forward. "Don Quixote," he said, bowing low. "I am the Knight of the Silver Moon and I challenge you to a duel."

Filled with excitement, Don Quixote rose from his seat. "I accept the challenge," he said.

They drew their swords and faced each other. Don Quixote raised his blade high and swept it through the air with a flourish. It seemed as if the Knight of the Silver Moon was only watching and waiting as Don Quixote danced around him, his sword slicing harmlessly, this way and that, through the air. But then, as Don Quixote came closer, the Knight of the Silver Moon suddenly lunged and knocked Don Quixote's sword clean out of his hand.

"You have won," said Don Quixote, bowing before him.

"I have," said the Knight of the Silver Moon. He took off his helmet – revealing himself to be none other than Carrasco, Don Quixote's old friend. "As I am victorious," Carrasco went on, "I want you to make me a promise that you will not unsheathe your sword for a whole year."

"I promise," sighed Don Quixote. "Come, Sancho Panza," he added, turning to his servant. "Our mission is at an end. We have united Kitri with her sweetheart. It is time we returned home."

And off they went, their adventure finally at an end.

This comic ballet is based on stories by
E. T. A. Hoffmann. With its tuneful, romantic music
by Léo Delibes, it is one of the great ballets
of the 19th century.

Coppélia

$\mathcal{I}$t was spring time, and everyone was gathered for a dance in the village square. As the dancers whirled across the cobbles, the mayor clapped his hands.

"Soon, our village will have a brand new bell," he announced. "To celebrate, we will hold a festival."

Everyone burst into applause and the mayor continued, "And what's more, all the couples who decide to get married on that day will be rewarded with a bag of gold!"

In the midst of the crowded throng, one of the dancers turned to her sweetheart. "That could be us, Franz," Swanhilda whispered.

"Yes, my love," said Franz, smiling. The band struck up, and they began to dance again, twirling across the village square.

"We're so lucky," said Swanhilda, as they danced. "Don't you think, Franz?"

Franz didn't reply.

"What are you looking at?" asked Swanhilda.

"What? Nothing!" said Franz.

But Swanhilda followed his gaze to the house of the inventor, Dr. Coppélius, where a girl sat motionless on a balcony, her eyes cast down to the book on her lap.

Dr. Coppélius was a strange man, but his daughter, Coppélia, was stranger still.

"You're looking at Coppélia again!" cried Swanhilda, filled with jealousy. "What's so special about her anyway? She might be pretty but she never moves! She never speaks! I've never even seen her leave that house. All she does all day is read, read, read."

"I have to go," Franz said suddenly.

With a quick kiss on her forehead, he hurried away from the dance, leaving Swanhilda alone, surrounded by laughing couples.

As Swanhilda walked home that night, she wondered if she could really marry Franz. He *said* he still loved her... but she was no longer sure.

Later, she crept back to the village square. She wanted to meet Coppélia for herself. But there was Franz, standing below Dr. Coppélius' balcony.

"Coppélia!" Franz called out. "Please, won't you talk to me? You know how I long to hear your voice."

He blew her a kiss up to the balcony, but the girl carried on reading.

"Coppélia, stop torturing me! Just look at me!" he begged.

Swanhilda fought back tears.

When Franz had gone,
she rushed across the
square, and stood under
the balcony herself.

"Coppélia?" said
Swanhilda. "Coppélia,
please speak to me."
But the mysterious girl
merely continued to read.

Swanhilda waved to her,
curtseyed to her, even danced
for her, but Coppélia refused
to acknowledge her.

"Fine!" snapped Swanhilda.
"*Don't* speak to me then.
See if I care!"

Still the wretched girl
said nothing.

"Swanhilda!" came a shout, "Come and help us!" It was her friends, holding bundles of flags and decorations for the festival.

Swanhilda hurried over. As she told them what had happened, Dr. Coppélius came out onto the street, and bustled past them. He was hunched over, eyes to the ground, his long black cloak swirling around his feet. Swanhilda longed to ask him about his daughter, but his face was set and grim. He had always been a mysterious figure, keeping himself to himself, never letting anyone into his house.

"Out of my way!" he barked and marched on, his feet striking hard and fast on the cobbles.

As he moved, there was a tinkling like metal on stone. Swanhilda's sharp eyes scanned the ground. She waited until the old man had disappeared from view, then she darted down, hands outstretched.

"Dr. Coppélius' key!" she cried, snatching it up, a plan already forming in her mind. She turned to her friends, beckoning them over, then whispered her plan.

"What do you think?" she said. "Shall we? Dare we?"

Her friends nodded. "How exciting!" they giggled. With peals of laughter, they left the village square and hurried home.

Late that night, the girls returned, softly stepping through the lamplight. Swanhilda put the key in the lock and pushed open the door. The other girls hung back, nervous, but Swanhilda beckoned them in. Together, they tiptoed up the stairs to Dr. Coppélius' workshop...

The air smelled strange, of sawdust and spices. At the far end of the room sat Coppélia, reading by lamplight.

"Coppélia? Coppélia?" said Swanhilda, approaching anxiously. "I want to talk to you. It's about Franz..."

Coppélia ignored her.

"Please," begged Swanhilda, stepping even closer. Then she gasped. "She's... not real! She's – she's a doll!"

"So *this* is Franz's perfect woman!" laughed her friends, nudging each other in amusement.

After that, they explored the workshop, pulling back dust sheets, peering into dark corners, discovering yet more strange inventions.

"Look!" said Swanhilda, turning a rusty key in a toy soldier. With a low, whirring sound, the soldier began to march across the room.

They wound up more and more toys – a laughing clown, a jack-in-the-box, a drummer boy playing rat-a-tat-tat on his drum, a dancing bear, a rocking horse and a monkey banging a tambourine. Swanhilda and the girls ran between them, and soon the room was alive with a strange procession of walking, dancing, jumping, leaping toys.

All at once, a white-haired figure dashed between them, roaring with rage.

"What do you think you're doing?"

The girls turned to see Dr. Coppélius rushing towards them, violently waving his walking stick.

"Out! Get out! All of you! NOW!"

With a flurry of feet, the girls flew about the workshop chased by Dr. Coppélius, until they dived through the door, down the stairs, laughing with relief as they reached the street once more.

"Idiots! Wretches!" Dr. Coppélius called after them, cradling Coppélia in his arms.

A thumping sound from the balcony made Dr. Coppélius turn. Gently, he placed Coppélia back in her chair and glanced all around.

"Who's there?" he called. Just then, he glimpsed a face at the window, ducking down to hide. "Ha! I've seen you, Franz!" he cried. "Come out! Come out! Don't be shy. Are you here to see Coppélia? She's often spoken of you."

"Really?" asked Franz, blushing.

"Tonight, you will meet," chuckled Dr. Coppélius. "First, let's have a drink."

And so, mumbling apologies, Franz shuffled into the workshop.

The doctor poured out a glass of rich, fragrant wine. "To young love," he said, handing Franz the glass. He watched, smiling, as Franz drank it down.

Franz looked at his empty glass, surprised at the strange taste of the wine. "That's odd..." he muttered, rising to his feet. He swayed for a moment and then staggered across the room, cannoning into the clockwork toys before sliding to the ground. Moments later, his eyes closed.

Dr. Coppélius hovered over him, his face lit with glee. "Yes!" he said in satisfaction, clapping his hands together. "And so it begins! Tonight, Coppélia will live! Now, where is my spellbook?"

Dr. Coppélius pulled out his spellbook, and brought Coppélia into the middle of the room.

He lifted up his arms and, in a thundering voice, he commanded: "Spirits! Take this young boy's spark of life. One young heart shall die and one shall be born. Bring Coppélia to life!"

Coppélia's eyes flickered open.

The doctor caught his breath.

Coppélia blinked, and slowly, very slowly, turned her head. Then she began to move, as if she'd only just discovered her body. She stood, and slowly began to dance around the workshop. Her movements were stiff and jerky, her legs kicking out, her hands like those on a clock, ticking through the air.

"It worked…" whispered Dr. Coppélius. A tear trickled down his cheek. "Franz is dead but you, my daughter, my best creation, are alive! I'm a genius! A magician! An inspirational inventor!" He waved his arms, only for Coppélia to become more alive still, jumping, leaping and twirling before his watery eyes.

She grew more graceful, dancing in flowing motions across the floor.

"A miracle!" gasped Dr. Coppélius. "My miracle."

Then she grew wild, mischievously setting off the clockwork toys, forcing Dr. Coppélius to chase after her, reprimanding as if she were a naughty child. He begged her to dance again, giving her a fan to perform a flamenco, a sash for an Irish jig.

Then, out of the corner of his eye, he saw Franz began to stir and rub his eyes. Dr. Coppélius looked at Franz and then back at the doll.

"But – " he began, flabbergasted.

The doll turned to him, and began to laugh. "It's me – Swanhilda!" she said. "Couldn't you tell?"

Drawing aside a dustsheet, she showed him his lifeless Coppélia. Dr. Coppélius grasped his doll, tears in his eyes.

"You tricked me!" he cried. Slowly, sadly, he

began to dance, Coppélia limp in his arms.

"Come," said Franz, grabbing Swanhilda's hand. "Come quick!"

"Oh," said Swanhilda. "Look at him – I can't leave him like this!"

"You have to," said Franz. "We can't stay in this crazy man's house."

And they leaped onto the balcony and began climbing down the ladder, leaving Dr. Coppélius alone in the workshop, with his strange collection of mechanical toys.

"I've been such a fool," said Franz, as they turned a corner. "I betrayed you and still you rescued me."

"I saw you climbing up to the balcony and I couldn't leave you. Yes, you are an utter fool," added Swanhilda, smiling. "But I love you."

The festival began the next morning. The new bell was unveiled, and in the midst of the cheering crowds were Franz and Swanhilda, who were to be married that very day.

As the priest began the marriage ceremony, there was an angry cry. A white-haired figure, dressed in a swirling black cloak, broke through the crowd. It was Dr. Coppélius, seeking revenge.

"You!" he said, pointing to the young couple. "You came into my house! You ruined my things! You tricked me! You must pay."

"We're sorry," said Swanhilda, leaving Franz's side. "We never meant to upset you."

"That's not good enough," Dr. Coppélius snapped. He was thinking of his doll, Coppélia, and how he would never see her come to life.

"I want to repair any damage we caused," said Swanhilda. "You must have my dowry. Here it is," she went on. "A bag of gold coins – all yours."

"Wait!" said Franz. "Don't give away your money. Dr. Coppélius must take mine instead."

The mayor stepped forward. "This is a wedding day," he said. "A time of celebration. *I* will pay Dr. Coppélius, on the condition that he joins us in the festivities."

Everyone looked at Dr. Coppélius.

"Is it agreed?" asked the mayor.

Slowly, Dr. Coppélius nodded his head.

After the wedding, the dancing began. Even Dr. Coppélius joined in, forgetting, for a moment, his dolls and his loneliness. And watching them all from the balcony was Coppélia, the same secret smile on her lips.

This beautiful ballet is danced to a magical score
by Pyotr Tchaikovsky. Based on a story by Alexandre
Dumas, it tells the story of a young girl's
wonderful Christmas adventure.

The Nutcracker

The Stahlbaums were busy preparing for their Christmas Eve party. Clara added the finishing touch to the decorations, placing a glittering fairy at the top of the Christmas tree.

"Magical!" said her mother.

Soon the room was buzzing with music and laughter, until the door opened and a hush fell. The last guest had arrived, a mysterious looking man, in a black cloak covered with stars.

Some of the children were scared of him, but Clara and her little brother Fritz ran forward in delight. It was their godfather, the wonderful toymaker, Herr Drosselmeyer.

First, he put on a puppet show. After that, to everyone's amazement, he brought in two life-sized, clockwork dolls – a bright orange harlequin, and a ballerina, all in pink.

As he wound them up, they opened their eyes and came jerkily to life, shrugging their shoulders and pointing their toes.

The children gasped as the ballerina began to twirl around the room, while the harlequin kicked his heels together in the air. He jumped and whirled around fantastically fast, while Herr Drosselmeyer looked on proudly. When the dance was over, he beckoned to his godchildren.

"And here are some presents just for you."

He presented Fritz with a toy mouse.

"Thank you!" said Fritz, beaming at his godfather.

But when he saw his sister's present, his face clouded with jealousy. Clara had been given a wooden soldier, complete with a braided jacket and a shiny black hat. What use would his sister have for a soldier? Surely it should belong to him!

"It's a nutcracker," explained their godfather. "Watch this..."

He placed a nut in the soldier's mouth and cracked it open with the soldier's jaws.

Clara took her Nutcracker and held it close. "Thank you, Godfather," she said. She loved the Nutcracker's handsome face, and the expression in his green eyes. For a moment, she almost thought he was smiling at her.

"*I* want a turn!" said Fritz, snatching the Nutcracker. He grabbed the biggest nut he could find and tried to force it into the soldier's mouth.

"No Fritz, don't!" cried Clara, but it was too late. The soldier broke in two and Fritz, angry and ashamed, ran away to hide. Clara picked up the pieces, and tried to bandage the Nutcracker with a ribbon from her dress.

"Don't worry," said her godfather softly. "Give it to me." And, with a mysterious wave of his handkerchief, the Nutcracker was once again as good as new.

Clara placed it below the tree to keep it safe, and joined her friends in a dizzy whirl of dancing.

The sky grew dark, the moon rose, and all too soon, the party was over. After the last guests had left, everyone went to bed. Only Clara was too excited to sleep. She tiptoed downstairs to fetch her Nutcracker from under the tree. She picked him up and cradled him in her arms. She didn't want to go to bed just yet, so she curled up beneath the tree. Soon, she was fast asleep...

DONG! DONG! Clara was woken by the grandfather clock striking midnight. It was eerily dark. The tree towered over her, its branches crackling and rustling. They seemed to be spreading, filling the room.

"The tree's growing!" Clara thought. "Unless... I'm shrinking?"

A sudden SCRITCH SCRATCH made Clara jump up in alarm. She turned to see hordes of huge, snarling mice scampering out of the shadows. They whirled silver swords as they ran.

"Help!" Clara cried.

To her astonishment, the Nutcracker sprang to life. He shouted a command at the wooden chest in the corner and an orderly line of toy soldiers came marching out, brandishing their muskets. They were led by a brave rabbit drummer, and followed by a line of cavalrymen on fine white horses, pulling a cannon.

Clara could only stare as the toy soldiers surged across the room, bringing their cannon with them, and growing bigger every moment, until they were the same size as their fearsome enemies, the mice.

"Into battle!" the Nutcracker cried, as the Mouse King rushed into the fray, waving a huge silver sword. A frantic battle followed.

Clara hid her face in her hands as the room filled with noise and smoke and the burnt, spicy smell of gunpowder. When the air cleared, only the Nutcracker and the Mouse King were left.

"Hand over the girl," ordered the Mouse King.

"Never!" replied the Nutcracker. But he was cornered. The Mouse King was about to overpower him. The Mouse King lunged forwards...

"Don't!" Clara screamed. She snatched off one of her slippers and hurled it at the Mouse King. It flew through the air and hit him right between the eyes. As he shuddered and staggered back, the Nutcracker seized his chance. He plunged his sword into the Mouse King's side, and the Mouse King dropped lifeless to the floor. The battle was over. The mice had been defeated.

When Clara looked back at the Nutcracker, he had changed. He was no longer a Nutcracker, or even a soldier, but a handsome prince.

"You saved my life," he said. "The Mouse King enchanted me and turned me into a nutcracker. Without you, I would have been imprisoned forever. Let me repay you. Let me take you on an adventure..."

With those words, the drawing room walls melted away and a snowy forest grew up around them. A flurry of snowflakes tumbled from the sky, swirling into delicate snow fairies. Clara gazed at them, spellbound, as they whirled around her. Soon she was surrounded by shimmering, white dancers, and she and the prince began to waltz along with them. As the prince lifted her up, and held her in the air, she felt as if she was floating.

Snow was falling thick and fast around them now. As Clara and the prince spun around and around, Clara could hear the sweet sounds of a choir singing Christmas songs, far away.

By the time the snow had settled, and the fairies had flitted away, a golden sleigh appeared. Herr Drosselmeyer stood beside it, resplendent in a deep blue cloak, beckoning to Clara and the prince. When they had taken their places, Herr Drosselmeyer clicked his fingers, and the sleigh was whisked up into the starry sky.

They soared through the night, flying over forests and frozen lakes until they reached a magical land. Clara had never seen – or smelled – anything like it before...

They floated past pink marshmallow clouds and over mountains topped with butterscotch ice cream. Far below were glistening rivers of toffee, lakes of lemonade and forests of lollipop trees.

They landed in a fragrant garden. Clara drank in the delicious scent of vanilla and roses. Then she bent down and looked at the flowers, and saw that they were made from spun sugar. Even the grass looked good enough to eat. But the most wonderful thing of all was the castle beyond the garden. It was made of frosted marzipan, with gingerbread turrets and chocolate tiles.

As Clara and the prince walked up to the door, a beautiful lady appeared. Clara had never seen anyone so elegant. Hundreds of tiny pearls hung from the tiara on her head, and her plum pink dress was embroidered with thousands of glittering diamonds.

"Clara," said the prince. "I'd like you to meet the Sugar Plum Fairy."

The fairy curtseyed gracefully and Clara tried to do the same.

"What brings you here?" the fairy asked.

So Clara told her the tale of the battle, the prince's bravery and the Mouse King's defeat.

The Sugar Plum Fairy clapped her hands with delight. "So it was *you* who saved the prince! The whole kingdom is grateful to you. This calls for a dance of celebration!"

She led them
through the castle, into a grand
banqueting hall. In the middle of the
room there was a long table, laden with
mouthwatering treats. There were silver
dishes heaped with candied fruits, and bowls
overflowing with jelly beans and chocolate
drops. The vaulted ceiling above Clara was held up
by columns of twisted barley sugar, and even the
floor was studded with rainbow candy canes.

As Clara and the prince took their seats on two
gingerbread thrones, a trumpet blast announced
the first dance – a dramatic Spanish dance known
as the fandango. The dancers were dressed in
velvety dark brown and made swirling moves, as if
they were stirring thick hot chocolate.

Next, Arabian dancers in soft silks swayed like
rising steam in a coffee dance.

Clara let the music wash over her as a chorus of flute players took to the stage. Their nimble feet moved as fast as their fingers. Clara was amazed by how they could play and dance at once.

Next came an athletic Chinese tea dance. Three performers leaped and tumbled around the stage, falling head over heels and then springing lightly back up into the air.

After that, Clara watched in astonishment as a

woman wearing a shimmering bronze dress and enormous, wide skirts took to the stage. As she swept around the room, she lifted up her hem and, to Clara's amazement, six children came running out from underneath it and began cartwheeling around the hall.

Then came a traditional Russian dance. Clara loved watching the dancers kicking high in the air with their bright red boots. When they raced away, she found herself swaying in time to a gentle waltz of ballerinas dressed as roses.

"Our celebration is nearly at an end," said the prince. He saw Clara's face fall. "But perhaps I could persuade the Sugar Plum Fairy to dance too," he added. "Would you like to see that?"

"More than anything," said Clara. So the prince stood up and invited the Sugar Plum Fairy to join him, as heavenly music began to play.

They dazzled everyone as they took to the floor. With each movement, the two dancers mirrored each other perfectly. It seemed as if they were moving, even breathing, as one person. Then the prince stood back, and the Sugar Plum Fairy danced alone, and Clara was entranced.

As the Sugar Plum Fairy spun around and around, she seemed as light as a butterfly, her feet hardly touching the ground. Watching her whirl and leap for pure joy, Clara imagined that *she* was the

one performing, that she was the one in that sparkling pink dress, that she was pirouetting with incredible grace.

Everyone in the hall was just as rapt as Clara, as the Sugar Plum Fairy wove her magic. When the dance finally came to an end, she looked radiant with happiness. The audience were instantly on their feet, cheering and clapping.

Clara didn't want the night to end, but now all the performers were lining up in front of her, bowing, curtseying and wishing her farewell.

"You were amazing," she told them. "I don't know how to begin to thank you..."

"The pleasure is all ours," replied the Sugar Plum Fairy softly.

Clara turned to the prince and gave him a hug.

"I don't ever want to leave. I don't want to say goodbye," she murmured, closing her eyes to hold back the tears.

"Perhaps one day, you will return," the prince told her. "But now your family is waiting for you, and you have Christmas day to celebrate. Who knows, you might have even more presents to open..."

But Clara knew she'd already been given the most precious gift she could ever receive. She would store her memories of this night in her heart, and treasure them for the rest of her life.

Outside, the sleigh was waiting. Clara climbed aboard, and it took to the skies once more. As she felt the air rush past her cheeks, she shut her eyes and pictured all the wonders she'd seen...

When Clara opened her eyes again, she was back at home, curled up under the tree. The prince was simply a wooden nutcracker under her arm. She looked up at all the decorations hanging in the tree – the candy canes, the wooden sleighs, and the fairy standing elegantly at the very top of the tree.

"Was it really all a dream?" she whispered to her Nutcracker. But he didn't answer. He just looked back and smiled.

Based on a Russian folk tale about a magical bird,
this ballet is a dramatic story of good against evil.
First performed in Paris in 1910, with music by Russian
composer Igor Stravinksy, it was an immediate success.

The Firebird

Prince Ivan stumbled through the forest. He had been out hunting and lost his way. Now night was drawing in and the twisted branches seemed to block his path at every turn. "Where am I?" he wondered. "And how will I ever get home?"

Then, ahead, he saw a wall, overgrown with moss and hanging ivy; and just visible beneath the cloak of greenery, a door...

He knocked, once, twice, but there was no answer. When he tried to knock again, the door creaked open, falling away from his touch. Hesitating only for a moment, Prince Ivan stepped through... into a magical garden, filled with apple trees. And from each tree, like tiny suns, hung shining golden apples.

"An enchanted garden," murmured the prince. "What sorcery is this?"

He wandered over to the nearest tree, where an apple hung from a low branch. He stretched out his hand towards the glowing orb of the fruit, but no sooner had he touched it than there was a fierce fluttering of wings and a bird swooped down from the branches. She was fiery red, a crest on her head, her long tail streaming like a comet. She seemed to dance around Prince Ivan, one minute coming closer, the next fluttering away, and for a moment he simply watched her, entranced. Then, unable to resist, he darted after her, snaring her in his arms.

The firebird struggled, desperate to break free. She twisted this way and that and, even though Prince Ivan muttered words to soothe her, she would not stay still.

Then she spoke. "Please! Let me go free."

"A magical bird in a magical garden," said Prince Ivan. "I am going to take you home and put you in a golden cage. You will be my most treasured possession."

"No!" cried the firebird, struggling harder still. "I belong here in this garden, where I guard the golden apples, not in a cage. You must not take me away from my home. Here," she added, plucking a blazing feather from her breast. "This is yours to keep. It is worth far more than this golden fruit. If you are ever in trouble, take it out and wave it through the air and I will come to your aid. Now, will you let me go free?"

"I will," said Prince Ivan, releasing his grip on the bird as he snatched up the feather.

The firebird fluttered her wings, as if shaking off the memory of her capture, and arched her long neck. Then she flew to the topmost branches of the trees, like a soaring firework against the darkening sky. She didn't once look back.

Prince Ivan tucked the firebird's feather beneath his belt and left the garden, setting off through the forest once more.

"This place must be full of magic," he thought. "It is best that I go home."

But he had a feeling he was moving only in circles, for it wasn't long before he came across another wall, this time with a wrought iron gate, its top studded with blackened spikes. Through the bars of the gate, Prince Ivan could see a towering castle, with turrets as twisted as the trees. Beneath the castle, in a clearing lit by moonlight, were thirteen princesses, in flowing white dresses, dancing between the flowers.

Silently, Prince Ivan slipped through the gate and stood watching them. And the more he watched, the more he felt his heart begin to beat faster and faster. For of all the princesses, there was one who caught his gaze and held it: a princess in a high crown and a red-ribboned dress embroidered with little yellow flowers.

She moved as if she were floating, gliding between the others, her arms outstretched and poised. Without thinking, Prince Ivan moved forward. He knelt before her and offered up his hands. She took them and he rose and they began a decorous dance: first circling and following each other, the other princesses looking on. Then they all began to dance together, weaving in and out of each other, as if caught in a spell by the moonlight. The princesses' white dresses shone star-bright and the dew in the garden sparkled like diamonds.

All night they danced, until at last Prince Ivan and the princess in the red-ribboned dress came together with a kiss.

"I love you," said Prince Ivan. "Come away with me and be my wife."

"I cannot," the princess replied. "My name is Vasilisa. I am trapped here. Long ago, we were all captured by the evil Koschei who owns this castle. He cast a spell over us so that we may dance by

night in the gardens, but at dawn, we are forced to return to the castle."

Even as she spoke, the dawn light began to creep across the sky. One by one, the princesses fled, back to the dark shadows of the castle.

"Come back!" cried Ivan. But in their wake came evil creatures, more bone than flesh, some bent low, swarming their way into the glade.

"Those are Koschei's demons! Beware!" cried the princesses as they fled.

The demons filled the glade, wicked smiles on their wicked faces. They surrounded Prince Ivan, circling and jeering.

Princess Vasilisa turned back, desperate to save the prince, but the demons drove her away. They circled ever closer, entrapping the prince in their ring. Prince Ivan tried to break through, but the demons were too many.

Then came a noise like the low rumble of thunder and another creature crept into the glade. Prince Ivan gasped. He knew this figure: it was Koschei the Deathless, an evil sorcerer, who was said to be immortal. What hope did he have of deafeating him?

Koschei's face was covered in a white mask and he wore a cobweb cloak with a pointed crown.

His body had no flesh, but was just black air and gleaming bones. He stalked towards Prince Ivan, hands raised, and declared, "I will turn you to stone!"

"Why?" cried Prince Ivan. "What have I ever done to you?"

"You dared to enter my garden," countered Koschei. "This is my realm. My magical realm." He raised his arms again.

Prince Ivan froze. He had no way to defend himself; there was nothing he could do against Koschei's magic. And then his eye caught sight of the flaming feather in his belt. He plucked it up and waved it boldly in the air.

At once, there was a rushing and a swooshing sound. The air was lit with fiery sparks and the firebird soared over the castle turrets.

She circled once above Prince Ivan, then she fluttered down to land in front of Koschei, small but fearless.

"How is she going to help me?" wondered the prince.

As if she had heard his silent question, the firebird began to flutter around the castle gardens – first left, then right, then high above the trees and low along the ground. Prince Ivan saw that Koschei and his army of demons were transfixed. Their eyes followed the firebird wherever she flew.

Then she circled back and touched them with her flaming feathers, and at last they began to move. With stiff, jerky limbs they imitated her, and she led them in her dance – back and forth and round and round...

The firebird drove them faster and faster, directing them with each flick of her wing, until

they were exhausted, stumbling on their feet or twitching on the floor. At last, they were still, captured in a deep, deep sleep.

Only then did the firebird approach Prince Ivan, beckoning him over to a tree stump. As Prince Ivan came near, he saw a golden chest, hidden within the hollow stump of the tree.

"Open the chest," commanded the firebird.

Prince Ivan heaved up the lid. There lay an egg, huge and gleaming, bone white as Koschei's mask.

"This," said the firebird, "is where Koschei hides his soul."

"What do I do with it?" asked Ivan, reaching down to touch it, its surface icy cold beneath his fingertips.

"You must smash it," said the firebird. "It is the only way to end Koschei's evil rule. Once he is truly dead, the princesses will be free."

On the firebird's command,
Prince Ivan lifted the egg high
above his head.

At this moment, Koschei
woke from his sleep.

"No!" he shouted, seeing
the egg in the air. "Don't!" he
cried, gasping, stumbling
over to where Prince Ivan
stood. "Put it back!
I command you to put
it back."

Prince Ivan looked once into the sorcerer's dark
eyes. Then he smashed the egg down hard onto the
rocky ground below.

Koschei opened his mouth to cry out, but no
sound came out. The great white egg split open
and, in a plume of green smoke, Koschei vanished

before the prince's eyes. All that was left of the sorcerer was his cobweb cloak, fluttering to the ground.

Prince Ivan gazed around the moonlit garden to discover that the demons and the twisted castle had gone, too. In place of the jutting turrets were tall trees, their branches waving in a gentle wind.

With a joyful cry the princesses came running, shouting, "We're free! We're free!"

Prince Ivan went down on bended knee before Vasilisa. "The spell has been broken at last," he said. "Will you marry me?"

"I will," replied Vasilisa, smiling.

They were married in the enchanted garden, beneath the golden apple trees.

The princesses danced to celebrate the wedding of Vasilisa and Prince Ivan. And above them all the firebird swooped and soared, her feathers glowing like the setting sun.

This romantic ballet was first performed in Paris in 1841. With haunting music and otherwordly settings, it tells a tragic story of love and betrayal.

Giselle

The warm autumn sun shone down on a little mountain village in Germany. Villagers twirled through the streets, hanging wreaths and garlands to celebrate the arrival of the grape harvest. Amid the merriment, a handsome man dressed in old, patched clothes lingered outside a house.

"Where is she?" he murmured to himself. He was waiting for his new girlfriend, a beautiful farm girl named Giselle.

"Sire," came a worried voice from behind. "I urge you to give up this act. You are Duke Albrecht of Silesia, and a distinguished nobleman. Please – take off this disguise and stop pretending..."

"Shush, Wilfrid," the handsome man snapped. "Someone will hear you! My name is Loys, and I am a humble farm boy."

"But..." Wilfrid replied weakly. "As your squire and confidant, I must insist... put an end to this foolish romance. You're betrothed to Bathilde!"

"That's enough, Wilfrid!" Albrecht scowled. "Giselle is about to arrive. Please, just go away."

Wilfrid sighed and reluctantly walked away.

A moment later, the door of the house flung open and a fair, rosy-cheeked girl appeared in the doorway. Albrecht gasped: it was Giselle, and she was looking lovelier than ever.

"Dear Loys," she cried, running into Albrecht's

arms. "I'm so sorry I'm late. Mother wouldn't let me leave. You know how she worries."

Albrecht kissed Giselle gently. "Darling Giselle, I'd wait forever for you." He stood back to admire her. Though she only wore a plain cotton dress and a few wild flowers in her hair, Giselle's beauty was enchanting. Her blue eyes sparkled like mountain dew, and her long, golden hair shone bright in the morning sun. "Come, let's dance."

Smiling shyly, Giselle took Albrecht's hand. Together, they spun gracefully through the trees, leaping over flowers and whirling under leafy garlands. After a while, Giselle rested her head on Albrecht's shoulder.

"I've never been happier, Loys," she whispered.

Just then, a dog barked and a man dressed in a rough wool cloak came striding towards them. It was Hilarion, the village gamekeeper.

"Giselle," Hilarion called out, "why are you dancing with *him*?" He shot Albrecht a dirty look. "I've told you not to trust him! Won't you dance with me?"

Giselle sighed. "Hilarion, enough. Loys is the man I love. Please leave us alone."

"You heard her," Albrecht snapped. "Giselle loves me, not you. Be gone!"

Hilarion frowned. "Fine. But this isn't the end of it." Then he turned to Giselle. "Gentle Giselle, I beg you, please don't trust this man." With that, he whistled for his dogs and set off into the forest.

Giselle didn't know what to say. "Loys, I..." she began. But her voice trailed off when all at once, Giselle and Albrecht found themselves surrounded by a group of merry, dancing villagers.

"Dance with us, Giselle!" cried a little girl. "The harvest celebrations have begun!"

Giselle smiled, and spun around on her tiptoes.
"Of course!" she replied, taking Albrecht's hand.

As everybody twirled together in the street,
Giselle and Albrecht soon lost
themselves in the dance.
Giselle extended her arms
gracefully as Albrecht
lifted her into the sky.

They'd only
been dancing a few
minutes, when a shrill
voice cut through all the
noise. "GISELLE!"

The music stopped, and
everybody stood still. Breathless, Giselle peered
through the crowd to see her mother, Berthe,
looking angry.

"I've told you a million times, Giselle," Berthe

scolded, wagging a finger at her daughter. "Dancing puts a strain on your weak heart!"

Giselle's cheeks flushed a rosy pink, and she let go of Albrecht's hand. "I'm sorry, Mother."

Berthe tutted. "If only you'd listen to your mother, instead of galavanting around with this *man*." She looked Albrecht up and down disapprovingly. "Come back to the house at once."

Giselle nodded, embarrassed, and followed her mother back down the street.

Albrecht watched her go. "I love you, Giselle," he called, blowing a kiss after her. But there was no reply. The door slammed shut and Giselle disappeared into the house.

Deep in the forest, Hilarion was seething. "There's something fishy about that Loys," he muttered, as he paced back and forth. "I'm going to find out what it is." He picked up his bag and marched back to the house where Loys was staying.

Standing outside, he whistled to his dogs. "Keep watch for me, boys," he said, nodding at them. Then he eased himself up through an open window at the back of the house.

Once inside, Hilarion let his eyes focus in the dim light. "What on earth…" he gasped.

There, laid out on the bed, was an exquisite set of hunting clothes: a rich velvet cloak, a pair of long leather boots and a large, golden hunting horn.

Hilarion's eyes grew wide. "So he *is* lying!" he muttered, shaking his head. "These aren't the clothes of a farm boy!" Snatching up the hunting

horn, Hilarion leaped back out of the window. "It's time to expose this so called *Loys*," he growled, "and win back Giselle once and for all!"

Back in the village square, glasses clinked as the villagers sat down to a great harvest feast. Albrecht sat quietly, picking at his food. He was just taking a bite of stew when a hunting horn sounded in the distance. Albrecht dropped his fork.

"The royal hunting party!" a villager cried, leaping out of her seat in excitement. "Quick, everybody prepare yourselves."

As the villagers set about clearing the table, Albrecht quietly edged back into the shadows. The other royals were the last people he wanted to see: the prince was likely to be joined by his daughter, Princess Bathilde. Albrecht had been so preoccupied with Giselle, he'd barely given his fiancée, Bathilde, a second thought.

"Make way, make way!" a voice bellowed down the street. "Make way for the prince, and his daughter, Princess Bathilde."

A group of footmen marched down towards the village square. There was a thunder of hooves behind them, and a group of luxuriously-dressed men and women appeared on horseback. Among them were the prince and Bathilde, draped in velvet and furs.

At the sight of the royals, a murmur of excitement rippled through the crowd.

"What a fine morning," the prince said, swinging down from his horse. "Just perfect for a hunt." He held out his hand to his daughter.

"Indeed, Father," Bathilde agreed, gracefully dismounting. "And oh! What a sweet little village this is! Let's stop here for a rest."

One of the villagers stepped forward and bowed. "Your Royal Highness, Princess Bathilde, welcome to our village. Please take a seat, and we will perform a harvest dance for you."

Smiling, Bathilde and the prince sat down on a bench as a group of villagers moved into position. Just as the fiddler struck up his first note, Giselle came dashing down the street. She'd spotted the royals arrive from her kitchen window.

"Oh, don't start without me," she cried. She curtseyed to the prince and Bathilde, and raced over to join the other dancers.

As the dance began, Princess Bathilde sat forward in her seat to watch. Before long, her gaze came to rest on Giselle. The beautiful farm girl moved with such grace, Bathilde was spellbound.

The dance finished, and Bathilde stood up to clap.

"Wonderful," she beamed, "just wonderful."
She pointed at Giselle. "You there, come over here.
I have something for you."

"Me?" Giselle put her hand on her heart.

"Yes, you." Bathilde replied. "Come here."

Shocked, Giselle walked over to Bathilde and
curtseyed graciously.

"You're a charming girl, and a talented dancer,"
Bathilde said. She unclipped a gold necklace from
her neck, and hung it around Giselle's. "I hereby
crown you Queen of the Harvest!"

Giselle flushed pink. "Thank you, ma'am,"
she whispered, too shy even to look up.

Bathilde smiled. "You're welcome."
She turned back to the prince. "Now,
Father. Shall we go?"

The prince stood up.
"Yes, let's. It's a glorious

day, and the hunt must go on!"

As the villagers waved the royal party off, Giselle clutched the precious gold necklace to her chest. Oh, how she longed to be as poised and sophisticated as Bathilde! She closed her eyes, reliving every moment of the dance again.

Just then, someone called her name. Giselle opened her eyes to see Albrecht, who had reappeared from the shadows.

"Loys, where have you been?" She smiled dreamily. "You won't believe what just happened..."

"I... um..." Albrecht began. He was about to launch into a long, elaborate lie, when Hilarion burst through the crowd.

"Liar!" Hilarion yelled, striding up to Albrecht.

Albrecht edged backwards. "Pardon me?"

"You're a liar!" Hilarion insisted. A group of villagers gathered around them to listen.

"What on earth are you talking about, Hilarion?" Giselle said. "Can't you just let it rest?"

Hilarion turned to Giselle. "This man, *Loys*, or whoever he claims to be – is not a farm boy," he spluttered. "He's a rich nobleman!"

Out of the corner of his eye, Albrecht caught sight of his hunting horn in Hilarion's hand. "N-n-o I'm not!" he stammered.

"We'll see about that," Hilarion replied. He put the horn to his mouth and blew hard. A loud noise blasted across the mountains. A few seconds later, another hunting horn responded nearby.

Hilarion smiled triumphantly. "Let's see if *this* will shed any light on the matter."

There was a clatter of hooves, and a party of noblemen and women came riding around the corner. It was the royal hunting party – they hadn't gone very far at all.

"Was that a hunting horn we heard?" the prince called out.

Bathilde pulled on her reins, and peered down at the crowd of villagers. "Albrecht!" she cried, spotting Albrecht at the front. "What are you doing here?" She jumped off her horse. "I haven't heard from you for days!"

"I-I-I..." Albrecht had no idea what to say or do.

Bathilde laughed, confused. "And why are you dressed like this?" She looked him up and down.

"Well, I..." Albrecht stammered.

Giselle laid her hand on Albrecht's arm. "Loys," she said. "What's going on?"

"Well, you see..." Albrecht's voice trailed off.

Bathilde looked from Giselle back to Albrecht. "Please explain, Albrecht," she said stiffly, the smile disappearing from her face. "Why are you wearing these dirty old clothes?"

Suddenly, Albrecht's expression changed. He laughed loudly. "Oh, darling. It's just a silly joke, really." He took Bathilde's hand in his. "Come on, I'll explain later. Let's head back to the palace."

As he began to march off, Giselle reached out to grab his other hand. "Where are you going, Loys?" she said, pulling him back. "What about us?"

Bathilde stared at Giselle in surprise. "Dear girl," she said. "I don't know who you think this man is, but I'm telling you now: he is Duke Albrecht of Silesia, and he is engaged to me!"

At these words, Giselle let go of Albrecht's hand and her face turned as white as snow. "Is this true?" she whispered.

Albrecht stood still, completely speechless.

"Loys?" Giselle insisted, her voice wavering. But her words were met with silence and, whimpering, she collapsed on the ground.

Giselle's mother, Berthe, pushed her way through the crowd. "Giselle!" she shrieked. "Your heart!" Then she glared at Albrecht. "What have you done?"

Giselle clutched her chest, and let out a long, agonizing moan.

Albrecht dropped to his knees. "I'm so sorry, Giselle," he said, gravely. "I'm not who I said I was. My name is Albrecht, and I am betrothed to Princess Bathilde."

Giselle looked up at him. "Please just answer me this," she whispered. "Do you love me?"

Albrecht sighed. "I love you, Giselle. But I am the Duke of Silesia, and I'm betrothed to be married..." His voice trailed off.

"I don't care who you are," she replied, her voice now so weak that Albrecht had to lean in to hear her. "But I will always love you."

A hushed silence fell across the crowd, as Giselle took one last breath and closed her eyes. Her heart had stopped beating.

Albrecht looked down at Giselle's body in shock. Slowly, it dawned on him what he'd done. "My darling Giselle!" he cried out, before pressing his lips to her cheek. "I'm so sorry!"

Deep in the forest, a blanket of mist shrouded the dank, mossy ground. A beam of moonlight fell upon a solitary mound of earth.

It was the place where Giselle had been laid to rest. Next to it sat Hilarion, deep in mourning.

"Oh, Giselle," he sobbed.

A dog howled in the distance, jolting Hilarion from his thoughts. "I'd better go," he mumbled. "Strange things happen in this forest at night."

As Hilarion stumbled off, silence fell over the forest. Above the trees, the moon grew brighter and brighter in the sky. Slowly, the blanket of mist parted, and a group of ghostly maidens appeared, all dressed in white. They walked hand in hand towards Giselle's grave.

"We are the spirits of abandoned brides," the maidens chanted, forming a circle around Giselle's grave. "We seek revenge on those who betrayed us

and left us to die."

One of the spirits wore a tiara in her hair. She spun into the middle of the circle. "I am Myrtha, Queen of the Spirits." She pointed at Giselle's grave. "I command you to wake up, Giselle!"

At those words, a dazzling halo of light appeared. Slowly, silently, a pale, willowy figure rose up from the earth. It was the figure of a beautiful girl – the spirit of Giselle.

Delicately, Giselle stretched out her arms and arched her neck. Then she swept over to join the other spirits. Myrtha nodded, and together the maidens began to dance beneath the silvery moon.

After a few minutes, the spirits grew still. A twig snapped – someone was walking nearby.

One by one, each maiden slipped back into the mist. Only the spirit of Giselle remained.

"Oh Giselle, forgive me, Giselle," came a voice. It was Albrecht, feeling his way through the darkness. He walked over to Giselle's grave and kissed the fresh earth. "Will you forgive me?" he murmured.

A dim light flickered above his head, and Albrecht looked up. Just out of arm's reach, he saw a pale, ghostly figure. It looked like Giselle.

"Giselle!" he cried out. "Is that you?"

"I am the spirit of Giselle," the spirit whispered, in a voice as gentle as the breeze. "I forgive you."

Albrecht gasped, and leapt up to embrace her. But before he could touch her, she vanished.

"Giselle! Where have you gone?" Tripping over the ground, he ran through the trees to find her.

On the other side of the forest, Hilarion was still trying to find his way home. As he lurched, frightened, through the mist, he came upon a group of pale, ghostly figures. It was the spirits – and they were looking for him.

"We are the spirits of abandoned brides," the maidens chanted, forming a circle around him.

Myrtha, Queen of the Spirits, pointed at Hilarion. "Dance for us!" she ordered.

"Go away!" Hilarion cried, frantically waving his arms. He tried to push past the spirits, but his body refused to obey him. Suddenly, he felt his legs begin to move, and he whirled around in a frenzied dance.

"Help me, someone!" Hilarion cried, prancing around like a puppet on a string.

Myrtha and the spirits did not answer, only watched silently.

Eventually, Hilarion let out a wail of exhaustion. "I can't go on," he groaned. Then, with a dull thud, he dropped to the ground.

Myrtha looked down at Hilarion and smiled coldly. "Now for the other one," she said, beckoning to the others. "Come!"

Hand in hand, the ghostly maidens swept through the trees. Soon, they came upon Albrecht, who was still searching for his beloved.

"Giselle?" he said, seeing movement in the mist.

"We are the spirits of abandoned brides," the maidens chanted, forming a ring around him.

Myrtha pointed at Albrecht. "Dance for us!"

"Get away from me!" Albrecht cried, thrashing his arms. He tried to run, but the power of the spirits was too strong, and he began to dance feverishly instead. "S-s-stop this at once," he panted, his body swaying back and forth.

Soon, Albrecht was so out of breath, he was struggling to speak. "Help me..." he said, hoarsely. "I c-c-can't breathe..." He was about to collapse when he felt someone touch his hand. He looked up to see the spirit of Giselle, standing next to him. "Giselle," he croaked. "Please – forgive me..."

Giselle smiled and kissed him softly. "I forgive you," she whispered.

Immediately, Albrecht felt his body relax. He took a long, deep breath. The strength of Giselle's love had diminished the spirits' power, and Albrecht's body was his own once again.

Just behind him, Myrtha let out a yowl of anger. "No!" She glared at Giselle. "You must avenge this fool! He abandoned you and left you to die."

But Giselle shook her head. "My love for him is true," she replied. "You have no power over either of us any more."

Myrtha's eyes flashed green with fury. But at Giselle's words, her power was gone. One by one, Myrtha and the maidens disappeared into the mist, and Giselle and Albrecht were left alone.

Albrecht gazed lovingly into Giselle's eyes. "Thank you for saving my life," he whispered, holding her hand to his chest. "Will you dance with me, darling Giselle?"

Giselle nodded, and laid her head on his chest. Together, they danced one final dance under the moonlit sky.

Albrecht closed his eyes as he held her body close to his. For a few fleeting moments, Giselle seemed more alive than ever.

Soon, dawn began to break. Birds began to wake up in their nests, as a faint yellow light flooded across the sky.

Giselle sighed deeply – her spirit was slowly beginning to fade.

"Don't leave," Albrecht whispered urgently, as Giselle's spirit gently slipped out of his arms. "Stay here with me. Please – I can't bear to be parted from you again, Giselle."

But Giselle shook her head, as a tendril of white mist began to curl around her body.

"My time is up, and I must go," she breathed. She was now no more than a fuzzy outline against the morning mist. "And you should find poor Bathilde. Make her happy, and remember: I'll never be far away, my love. Listen out for me on the breeze."

As Giselle's spirit finally disappeared, Albrecht found himself alone once again. He broke down into a sob. "Giselle! Come back to me!"

Just then, a soft breeze blew all around him, and the hairs on his neck stood on end.

"I love you," the breeze seemed to whisper.

Albrecht closed his eyes and felt it against his skin. Through his tears, he began to smile. Giselle had forgiven him and, although she was gone, she would live on in his memory forever.

With music that evokes the ever-changing moods of the sea, this ballet tells the tragic tale of a water nymph who falls in love with a mortal.

Ondine

The fountain in the town courtyard rose and fell in a glittering arc. A nobleman named Palemon sat watching it, while beyond, a scented pine forest ran down to the sea. There, on the shore, fishermen in wooden boats cast out their nets, praying for a good day's catch.

Palemon was thinking of Berta, his future wife. Their wedding was not far off, but he felt only dread, rather than happiness.

Perhaps it was because of their constant quarrels. Only this morning, after an argument, Berta had thrown his necklace back at him when he'd offered it to her, and waltzed off in anger. Was that why he wasn't more excited?

Or perhaps it was because he felt as if his whole life was being mapped out before him, and he wanted something more, something different. He vowed not to think of Berta again today, but instead to sit back and enjoy the sunshine.

He looked across the square, and there, stepping out from the fountain, seeming to come from the water itself, was a girl – her dress cascading like a waterfall, her steps across the cobblestones as fast and fleeting as falling rain. She shivered as she ran, unfolding her arms and waving them through the air, as if feeling the breeze against her skin for the first time. Her eyes darted this way and that, taking in the paved streets, the sunlit buildings, the flowers in the window boxes.

Casting her eyes behind her, the girl caught sight of her shadow and gasped. She ran a few more steps and glanced back, surprised, it seemed, that her shadow was following. She danced across the courtyard, laughing and skipping, as if she'd made a new-found friend.

Palemon was entranced. Her laughter was as light and mischievous as a child's. The way she moved was beautiful, graceful, like a dolphin cresting the waves. He rose to his feet and the girl caught his glance.

"I am Palemon," he said. "A nobleman of this land. What is your name?"

"Ondine," the girl replied. He could tell by the way she hesitated that he made her somehow frightened.

"I won't hurt you," he said. "Please," he added, "will you dance with me?"

Entranced, Ondine flowed into Palemon's arms and they turned and whirled, spinning across the ground together. But every now and then she would slip from his grasp, darting away from him, a minnow in a brook. Her flesh was cold to the

touch, as if it had been formed far from the sun.
Her hair, streaming down her back, reminded
him of waterweeds, flowing with the tide. She felt
other-wordly in his arms; a secret from somewhere
unknown and undiscovered.

Then, all at once, Ondine stilled, her eyes
alighting on the jewel in his necklace. Curious, she
reached for it and pulled it away. She held it up to
the light and turned it over in her hands.

Palemon watched her, wondering at the
intensity of her gaze, the way she looked at the
necklace as if she'd never seen one before.

She skipped away with it, holding the glinting
jewel up to the sun, and then returned, replacing it
carefully around his neck. For a moment, the palm
of her hand rested against Palemon's chest – and
she fell back in surprise at the steady rhythm she
felt there...

For Ondine was a water sprite, a creature of the sea, and she had no heart and no soul. Never before had she felt a beating heart, the strong quick pulse of human life... and she loved it. She loved the warmth and the strangeness, yet at the same time she felt afraid.

She turned from Palemon and ran, diving this way and that, until she came to the forest that spilled its way down to the sea. Palemon ran after her – and unknown to them both, Berta was following. She had been watching all the while, furious that her fiancé should have eyes for another.

In a forest glade, at the water's edge, Palemon approached Ondine once more. And this time, her longing overcame her fear. She was drawn to him, wanting something other than the crashing waves and the vast empty depths of the sea...

She placed her hand gently over his beating heart once more.

"Marry me?" Palemon heard himself say, the words out before he could stop them, all thoughts of Berta flown from his head. He spun her around the glade, feeling as if he'd been bewitched.

"Yes, I'll marry you," said Ondine, enraptured by the dance, captured by her first feelings of love.

But the Lord of the Sea was listening, and he would do anything to stop the marriage of a water nymph to a man. As Ondine made her promise, he rose from the sea, in a burst of spray and foam, wearing a cloak of green. His skin shone iridescent blue, his eyes were stormy and he was swelling with anger.

"Ondine, you cannot marry Palemon," he commanded. "If you married him, you would gain a human soul. And if he betrayed you? Do you know what would happen then?"

Fearfully, Ondine shook her head.

"If he betrayed you, you would die," said the Lord of the Sea. "You must leave him, and return to us, where you belong."

Other water nymphs rose above the surface of the sea. "Come back to us, Ondine," they called, beckoning to her. "This is where you belong."

"No – I belong to the land now," Ondine declared. "Palemon will be faithful to me. I'll marry him, whatever you say."

Palemon and Ondine were married that day, by a hermit who lived in the forest, while Berta watched, broken-hearted, from behind the trees, her face twisted in bitterness and anger.

"I thought he loved me," she wept. "Palemon is

mine! That sea witch has stolen him with magic. I will do everything I can to get him back."

After the wedding was over, Palemon asked for his boat to be made ready in the port.

"We'll sail around the coast," he said to Ondine, "in celebration of our marriage."

At first, the waves lapped calmly against the sides of the boat. The sun shone, and the waters of the warm sea sparkled and glittered.

They sailed further and further from the shore. The white sails flapped in the breeze, then began to billow as the wind picked up.

Standing on the sun-soaked boards of the boat, Ondine shivered. She felt it in her bones – the rising swell of the Sea Lord's rage. Little by little, she saw the waves get bigger. She saw the storm clouds gather low in the sky, great black masses on the horizon, full of fury and rain. She felt the boat begin to rock, this way and that, so that she and Palemon were pitched roughly from side to side.

Palemon held on tight to her. "Don't worry," he said. "I'll get us through this."

He wrestled with the sails, trying to steer the boat through the storm. But Ondine stared at the crashing waves in despair. She saw the other sea nymphs leap from the spray and vanish again beneath the waves. She glimpsed the hand of the Sea Lord, stirring the churning waters. The sea was his weapon and Palemon was powerless against it.

The wind was blowing harder and harder now. The clouds pressed close against them, and the air was thick with mist, heavy and opaque. The sea rose and frothed and rose again, until great waves were crashing up, and up, and over them. The boat was tossed by the waves as helpless as a leaf in a gale.

Ondine

Ondine

Ondine slid to the side of the boat.

"No!" Palemon cried.

But Ondine knew what she had to do. The storm
would go on until she returned home. The Lord of
the Sea would stop at nothing to ensure her return.
Ahead lay black rocks, their sharp points thrusting
out of the water, and the boat was heading towards
them. Palemon was sure to drown. She had to go.

When the next wave came, Ondine went with
it, letting herself be sucked down, down, down
beneath the waters.

She heard Palemon's cry as she went. She saw
him reach after her, and then she was claimed by
the sea as its own.

For a moment, Palemon looked on in despair.
Then, he too was thrown in the water as the boat
smacked against the rocks. The wood splintered
and cracked. Palemon clung to the wreckage.

He thought this was the end, that he would be dragged under at any moment – and now that he had lost Ondine, he didn't care. But, as if by magic, the storm calmed as swiftly as it had begun. The great black clouds rolled back, the waves dropped and the sun shone once more. Palemon bobbed on the surface and felt himself being carried gently back to the shore...

There, Berta was waiting for him. She had watched the storm from the cliffs and seen Ondine disappear beneath the waves. With a smile on her lips, she had whispered, "Ondine is gone. Palemon will be mine once more."

Then she had wrapped her blood-red scarf around herself and hurried down to the beach, to pull Palemon from the water.

"All is forgiven," she told him. "We will be married now, just as we should have been before."

The wedding of Berta and Palemon was
arranged as a grand affair. It was to take place in
his family's palace on the cliff tops. All the nobles
in the land would be there, dressed in their finest
clothes. Berta's heart beat with excitement; finally
she was going to be married.

Palemon moved among his guests as if in a daze.
His movements were slow and he dragged his feet.
He was marrying Berta only because he no longer
cared what happened to

him. Without Ondine,
his life seemed empty
of meaning. He had
glimpsed another
world, only to have it
snatched away from
him, with no hope of
finding it again.

Strangely, after his vows to Berta had been made, as the guests took to dancing, he felt himself being watched. He turned and stared. Ondine stood before him, as willowy as he remembered, her hair falling in waves, her arms swaying, her steps as light as ocean spray.

"Are you haunting me now?" he cried. "Are you a ghost? Or am I dreaming?"

Ondine kept looking at him, her face stricken with sorrow. "I am not a ghost," she said. "How could you betray me like this?"

"I only married Berta because you were gone," he said. "I thought I had lost you forever."

"It's too late," Ondine replied, sadly. "The Sea Lord will have his revenge and so will my fellow water nymphs. Everyone here is in danger."

The next moment the palace walls shook as the sea crashed against the cliffs. Palemon rushed to the window. Below, the waters were once again being whipped into a terrible storm.

"The storm is the price for my betrayal?" Palemon asked.

Ondine nodded. After that, all chaos broke loose. The sea surged over the palace walls, blasting away glass and stone. The wedding guests screamed in fear and confusion, scattered on a tide of the Sea Lord's making, until only Palemon and Ondine were left.

"I have given up my human soul," Ondine said. "I am once again a water nymph, without a beating heart."

"And still, I long to kiss you," Palemon replied.

"And still, I wish you were mine."

He came towards her. The resignation on his face showed he knew his fate, even desired it, and Ondine could no more hold back than Palemon. Their lips met in their first kiss – but it was a kiss of death.

Palemon fell to the ground. Ondine wrapped him in her arms and, on the next wave, she carried him with her, back to the watery depths, where the Lord of the Sea was waiting.

"Make him live again," Ondine cried.

"Impossible," said the Sea Lord. "I will do one thing for you, however." And he gazed at Palemon until his body turned to stone, a lifeless statue, a memorial to Ondine's first and only love.

'La Sylphide' means 'the sylph' – a spirit of the air.
A strange tale of love and enchantment, this ballet
was first choreographed by Filippo Taglioni in 1832.
His daughter, Marie, danced the role of the sylph.

La Sylphide

*J*ames was dozing in an armchair in a grand old Scottish hall. He'd stayed up late the night before and hadn't even made it to bed. Now it was dawn on his wedding day, but he wasn't dreaming of his wife-to-be, Effie. He was dreaming of a beautiful, dancing sylph – a spirit of the air, so light and so free...

A soft kiss on his forehead woke him and there she was, the sylph herself, as beautiful as in his dream and dancing away from him.

"Wait!" cried James. "Who are you? Am I still dreaming? Don't leave me!"

But the graceful sylph darted to the fireplace and disappeared up the chimney, above the cold ashes.

James gazed at where she had been, rubbed his eyes and gazed again.

Nothing.

He called to his friend, who was slumbering in another chair. "Gurn! Did you see that? Oh Gurn, WAKE UP!"

"See what? Where?" mumbled Gurn sleepily. "What's going on?"

"An enchanting sylph, in this room," James said. "The most beautiful creature you could imagine..."

"Effie's more beautiful than anything," said Gurn gruffly, "and you don't need to imagine her. You're marrying her today!"

At that moment, a pretty young woman in a

tartan dress skipped into the room.

"Effie!" cried Gurn, jumping up to greet her.

Effie smiled at her friend, then turned to her fiancé. "Oh James," she said softly. "Can you believe that in two hours we shall be married?"

James looked at Effie fondly. Soon they were surrounded by Effie's bridesmaids, chattering excitedly and wishing them well.

James stole a quick glance at the fireplace, and was surprised to see an old woman in a dark cloak beside it. She was warming her hands by the glowing embers, which only minutes ago had been as cold as stone.

"What are you doing here?" he shouted.

"I'm only an honest fortune-teller," croaked the old woman, a glint of mischief in her eyes.

"A fortune-teller!" cried the bridesmaids. They quickly crowded around her, holding out their hands eagerly.

"Tell me my fortune."

"And mine."

Effie waited her turn. "What about our fortune?" she said shyly, holding out her hand and urging James to do the same.

The old woman studied their palms closely, then

looked up at Effie. "You are soon to be married," she said slowly. "But not to him."

Effie's eyes widened and her smile vanished.

"That's preposterous!" blurted James, snatching back his hand.

"Now it's my turn," spoke Gurn, striding up to the old woman and holding out his hand.

"Ahhh," said the old woman knowingly, examining Gurn's palm, then turning to Effie. "This is the man you shall marry."

Gurn gasped. He couldn't help beaming with delight, but everyone else was horrified.

"That's enough!" shouted James, bundling the old woman up in her cloak and pushing her towards the door. He returned to the fire and stood with his arms folded, trying to control his anger.

Gurn was nowhere to be seen. He'd slipped out of the room.

It was the bridesmaids who comforted Effie and led her back to James. He softened when he saw her, taking her small hand in his. "That woman's crazy," he assured her. "Don't believe a word she says. We're getting married in less than two hours and nothing can stop that!"

Effie let out a little sigh and allowed herself to smile again. Of course James was right. They wouldn't let a crazy old woman spoil their day.

"Come on," she called to her friends. "We have a wedding to prepare for!"

"I'll come too," said James following them to the wide, wooden staircase.

"Oh no you won't," Effie laughed. She blew James a kiss and ran up the stairs after the other girls.

James was left alone with his thoughts. He turned to the empty fireplace and sighed. Then a movement at the window caught his eye and there

she was again – the sylph
from his dreams!

"I'm imagining things,"
he told himself firmly.

But slowly and silently
the window opened, and
the sylph stepped lightly
into the hall.

Once again, James was
spellbound by her beauty.
He watched, entranced, as
she spun her magic around
him, twirling, swooping,
teasing...

At last, she spoke. "I love you," she said simply,
"and I think you love me too."

"But I can't love you!" cried James, torn. "I'm
marrying Effie today."

"You can love me, and you do," the sylph replied.

She twirled away from James and he couldn't help following her. They danced together around the hall, as if it was the most natural thing ever.

Then James spotted Gurn in the doorway. How long had he been there? Had he seen the sylph? Hoping he hadn't, James quickly ushered her into an armchair and draped a blanket over her. But it was too late...

"Effie!" cried Gurn urgently. "Effie come quickly. James is cheating on you!"

Footsteps clattered down the staircase as Effie and her bridesmaids came running.

"Whatever do you mean?" demanded Effie.

"Look, I'll show you!" cried Gurn. He bounded up to the armchair and whisked off the blanket to reveal... nothing. "But..." he protested.

"Oh Gurn," sighed Effie. "That's not funny."

James breathed a long, low sigh of relief.

The hall began to fill with wedding guests and a band of musicians struck up a lively tune. Soon everyone was jigging around the room, dancing intricate Scottish reels and making circles around the bride and groom.

Effie beamed at James and James smiled back. He told himself that his love for Effie was real and that the sylph was only in his imagination. But then he spied the sylph again, weaving between the guests. No one else noticed her, but James saw her everywhere. She was tempting him to follow her, to leave his wedding, to leave his life behind...

Then the moment came for the bride and groom to exchange rings. James tried to fix his eyes on Effie. He held out her ring, but the sylph swiftly snatched it from him and darted out of the hall. Without hesitation, James fled after her.

"James!" howled Effie in disbelief.

Meanwhile, in a misty forest glade, the old woman was warming herself by another fire.

She raised her hands above a bubbling cauldron and chanted:

"Magic veil
Do not fail.
Trick young James
And ruin his games."

Carefully, she pulled a lacy white veil from the cauldron, then scurried into the dark undergrowth.

A group of sylphs flitted among the forest branches. Soon the enchanting sylph from the wedding joined them, followed by the besotted James. He longed to hold her in his arms, but she was a spirit of the air and she kept slipping away.

James looked on with growing frustration as the sylph joined her sisters, weaving their way though the trees.

"I can help you," croaked a voice.

Turning in surprise, James saw the old woman move out of the shadows.

"Take this veil," she went on, holding out the lacy material. "Place it around the sylph's shoulders, and she will be yours forever."

James eyed the old woman suspiciously. Then he noticed in alarm that his beloved sylph was rapidly

disappearing from view. He grabbed the veil and ran after her.

Moments later, Effie arrived in the forest glade with Gurn.

"How could he just run away like that," she said. "And from our wedding!"

"Better than deserting you *after* the wedding," said Gurn, trying to comfort her.

"Ah, the happy couple," crowed the old woman. "I said you would marry each other."

"No," Effie said quickly. "You don't understand..."

"Oh, don't I?"

"She's right, Effie," said Gurn. "You were never meant to be with James. He can never love you the way *I* do."

There was a glimmer of happiness in Effie's eyes as Gurn took her hand and got down on one knee.

"Will you marry me?" he asked hopefully.

James knew nothing about Gurn's proposal.

All thoughts of Effie were pushed far from his mind as he stumbled after his beloved sylph. "Wait for me!" he called breathlessly. "I've found a way we can be together."

The sylph led James in a playful game of chase. He tried in vain to drape the veil over her, but she was too quick from him. Eventually, he managed to drape the lacy material around her shoulders. But when James reached out finally to embrace her, the veil slipped to the ground, revealing nothing but thin air. The sylph had simply disappeared.

"Nooooooo!" howled James.

"You've been a fool," came the familiar voice of the old woman. "You should have treasured what you had, rather than chase after a fantasy. Now you've ended up with nothing."

The sound of church bells drifted across the

forest, mingled with distant laughter. Through the trees, James could just make out a wedding procession, snaking its way along the forest path.

"That should have been me," he moaned, sinking to the ground.

Leading the procession were the newly-weds, Effie and Gurn, walking arm-in-arm and rejoicing on the happiest day of their lives.

This comic ballet – also known as 'The Wayward
Daughter' – was created by French choreographer, Jean
Dauberval. He is said to have been inspired by a painting
he saw, of a young girl being told off by her mother.

La Fille Mal Gardée

*D*awn was breaking. In the farmyard outside Lise's house, the roosters crowed and the hens clucked. Lise crept outside, looking for the man she loved.

"Colas? Colas?" she called. But he wasn't there. As a token of her love, she left him a pink ribbon wrapped around the gatepost, then went sadly back into the house.

Moments later, Colas appeared. He tied the bow to his staff and called up to the window.

"Lise! It's me – come out!"

But Lise didn't appear at the window. Instead, Colas found himself gazing up at the face of Lise's furious mother, Simone.

"Away with you, peasant boy! I don't want to see you anywhere near my daughter! Scram!"

Lise's mother banged the window shut, and turned to her daughter.

"Oh, don't look like that!" she said, as she saw her daughter's downcast face. "Colas is a nobody. Forget him! There's sweeping to be done, cakes to be baked, butter to be churned! Stop your daydreaming and get to work."

So Lise started her household chores, while her mother sat reading.

"I've got my eye on you," her mother warned.

But a few minutes later, Lise smiled as she heard one of her best-loved sounds – the low rumble of her mother snoring.

Lise raced outside. Colas was waiting for her behind a tree. Under the bright blue sky, they chased each other around the field, and then danced together. They wove the ribbon between their hands, and spun around, winding the ribbon around their waists.

When Simone woke up, yawned and clomped out into the yard, Colas ducked behind a hedge.

"The butter's not churned! The hall hasn't been swept!" barked Simone crossly. "What have you been up to?"

"I was... looking at a bird?" said Lise.

Her mother's eyes narrowed. "If you've been messing around with that good-for-nothing Colas, I swear, I'll make you regret it... and don't think for a second I won't find out!"

"Colas? Who's Colas?" said Lise, trying to look as innocent as possible. It didn't work. Her mother dragged her back into the house.

"Who's Colas?! What kind of fool do you take me for? Forget Colas! You are going to marry Alain! And why's that?"

"Because you don't care about my happiness," said Lise.

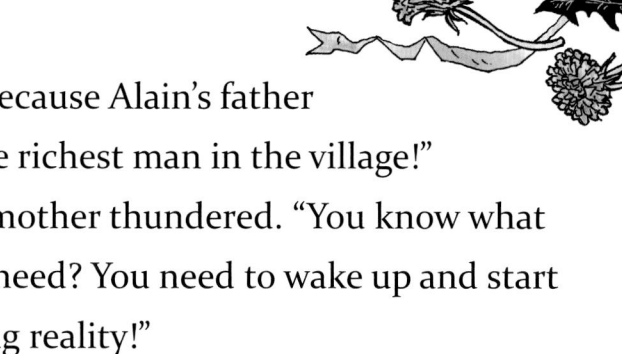

"Because Alain's father
is the richest man in the village!"
her mother thundered. "You know what
you need? You need to wake up and start
facing reality!"

Just as Simone aimed a loaf of bread at her
daughter's head, there was a knock at the door.
Simone froze. Lise tiptoed to the window.

"It's Alain and his father!" said Lise, horrified.

"Alain and his father," said Simone breathlessly.
She smoothed her dress, dabbed on some perfume
and threw open the door.

"Welcome!" she cried. "How wonderful to see
you both."

As Simone ushered them inside, Lise gave Alain
the biggest smile she could muster, though it was
so weak it was almost invisible. Standing before her
was the man she was destined to marry, wearing

a straw hat, a pair of bright green trousers and a lurid gold waistcoat. In one hand, he was clutching a wilting bunch of dandelions. In the other, he held a bright red umbrella. After thrusting the flowers into her hands, he opened the umbrella, crouched on the floor, and disappeared underneath it.

"Don't mind Alain," said his father, breezily, giving his son a prod. "He's just a little shy. Say hello to Lise, Alain."

Alain stood up again and smiled half-heartedly at Lise. "We're just off to the harvest picnic," his father said. "Why don't you join us?"

"We'd love to!" said Lise (who knew Colas would be there too).

As soon as they arrived at the picnic, Lise flitted off to dance with Colas.

"This is what happiness feels like," she thought, as they whirled around.

"Lise! LISE!"

Her mother tugged her away from Colas. "You must dance with Alain!"

"I'm not sure if that's even possible," said Lise, pointing. Everyone else was dancing in pairs, but Alain was waltzing with his umbrella. "He looks quite happy as he is," she ventured.

"Dance with him," her mother hissed, "or I'll lock you in your room for a week!"

So Lise tried to dance with Alain, although his steps were a little hard to follow. He seemed to be dancing to a different tune, one that existed only in his head. One moment he leaped like a frog, the next he scuttled sideways like a crab. Then, in a moment of inspiration, he decided to pick Lise up and carry her around the village.

Lise was quietly wondering how she would survive the rest of the dance, when Alain caught

sight of something that made him forget her
instantly. One of the village boys was playing a
recorder. He loved recorders! He dropped Lise on
the ground, plucked the recorder out of the boy's
hands and started to play a tune.

Alain's playing was as expert as his dancing. Soon
everyone was yelling for him to stop. But Alain
ignored them all. When one of the village boys
grabbed the recorder back, he threw himself on the
ground and started to wail.

"How can I marry him?" said Lise. "He's like a
little child!"

"Oh, nonsense!" said her mother. "Alain is a
gentleman. He's got a lovely..." For a moment
she paused, lost for words. "...umbrella!" she
announced, pleased to have remembered one
of Alain's best qualities. "And a truly delightful
income. So stop gawping at that farm boy Colas!

Honestly, my girl, I've half a mind to send you home right away."

"Mother, why don't you show everyone your clog dance?" replied Lise, sweetly. The clog dance was her mother's old party trick. Lise hoped it would cheer her up.

"I couldn't possibly," said Simone. "I haven't danced it in years."

"Please," begged Lise. "You know how much everyone loves it..."

"Well, if you insist," said Simone. Then she tossed her shoes into the air and put on her bright yellow clogs.

Clickety-clackety-click. Tap! She stomped her way across the square.
Clickety-clackety-click.
Tap! Now everyone was joining in.

Clickety-clackety-click! She gave a high kick and
everyone cheered. *Clickety-click! Kick!*

At the end, everyone burst into applause, apart
from one elderly villager who'd been a little put
out by one of Simone's clogs whizzing right past
her nose.

"You were wonderful!" said Lise, when Simone
had taken a bow. She hadn't seen her mother
so merry for years.

Then it was time for the dance Lise liked best. The whole village joined in, whirling around the maypole. Lise hoped her mother wouldn't notice Colas holding her hand as they danced.

The dance might have carried on all afternoon, if it hadn't been for a sudden rumble of thunder. The sky darkened.

Rain lashed at the maypole. Then a gust of wind swept through the village, taking the maypole with it. Everyone shrieked and ran for cover, while Lise and Colas sheltered together under a tree.

"Please can you explain something to me," said Lise. "My dress is torn. The party's ruined. I'm freezing and covered in mud. So why am I so wonderfully happy?"

Colas answered her with a kiss. "Would you like to join me for the next dance?" he asked.

"I'd love to," said Lise, and they danced together in the rain.

Meanwhile, Alain was less happy. The storm was threatening to take away his most precious possession – his umbrella. He clung onto it, as he was flung this way and that.

"Help! Help! I'm flying!" he shrieked, as his feet left the ground. Who knows where he would have ended up, if his umbrella hadn't caught in the branches of a tree.

When Lise arrived home, her mother was not impressed.

"You look like a drowned rat," she said. "You can't get married looking like that!"

"Married?" said Lise.

"Yes, child. Married. Alain and his father are going to arrive in a couple of hours for your wedding."

"Wedding?" repeated Lise, horrified.

"Yes, your wedding! Go and clean yourself up.

And don't even think of running away. I'm going out, and I'm locking the door."

When her mother had left, Lise stood in the empty kitchen. She couldn't bear to think about the wedding. Instead, she thought about Colas... What if she could marry Colas instead of Alain?

She started to dance around the room. They'd live in the village. One day they'd have children. Just two, or three, or five...

"I'm Lise," she said. "This is my husband Colas, and these are our seven children –"

"Seven?!"

"Colas!" she shrieked, shocked to discover him standing behind her. "How did you get in here?"

"Love always finds a way," he said. "Also, one of the windows was open. Let's run away!"

Lise ran to Colas and kissed him. But before they could make their escape, they heard the sound of the key in the lock.

"It's Mother! Quick, into my bedroom!"

Simone was humming as she came through the door. "Oh, I do love a wedding," she said. But when she saw her daughter, her face fell.

"Come on, get into your dress!" she said.

"But I *can't* marry Alain," Lise told her.

"You can and you will," said Simone.

She pushed Lise into her bedroom and locked the door.

A few minutes later, Alain and his father arrived.

"Your bride awaits you," said Simone, handing Alain the key to Lise's bedroom. "Let her out."

So Alain opened the bedroom door, to see Lise... And Colas. Kissing.

"No!" cried Simone.

La Fille Mal Gardée

"No!" wept Alain. It was awful. It was almost as bad as the time that someone had taken away his precious recorder.

"Please," begged Lise, holding Colas' hand. "Let us be married. We love each other."

Simone looked at her daughter. Then she looked at Alain, who had once more taken refuge under his umbrella. She had thought that Alain's riches would one day bring her daughter happiness. But with Colas beside her, it was clear that Lise had everything she wanted.

"Fine," she sighed. "If you really think it's best."

Lise rushed into her mother's arms. "Thank you, thank you!" she cried joyfully, as Colas whooped with delight.

Even Alain seemed to get over his heartbreak quite quickly. He walked around the village and asked Lise's friends, one by one, if they would like

220

to marry him instead. When they all said no, he looked slightly relieved.

The whole village took to the fields to dance in celebration, and the house was empty and quiet... Until Alain returned in a frantic state. He had lost his one true love. But after a few desperate moments, he danced for joy. He had found his beloved umbrella.

Shakespeare's play 'Romeo and Juliet', a tragic tale
of star-crossed lovers, inspired this ballet. With music
by Sergei Prokofiev, it is one of the most passionate
ballets of the 20th century.

Romeo and Juliet

In the beautiful Italian city of Verona, there lived two noble families who hated each other passionately. All Montagues and Capulets were bitter enemies – and had been for as long as anyone could remember.

Early one morning, a young man named Romeo Montague wandered down a street with his friends, Benvolio and Mercutio.

"Oh Rosaline," Romeo sighed, lost in thought. "Why don't you love me?"

Benvolio – another Montague, and Romeo's cousin – patted him on the back. "Forget about Rosaline, Romeo," he said. "She's a Capulet, and a great enemy of ours. Besides, there are plenty of other girls out there!"

"He's right," Mercutio agreed. Mercutio and Romeo had been friends since they were very young, and Mercutio knew that his friend was easily distracted by girls. "Stop daydreaming about her, Romeo, and move on."

Romeo shrugged. He'd been seeking the attention of Rosaline for weeks, but she'd barely batted an eyelid at him. He couldn't care less that she was a Capulet.

The three young friends strolled into the town square, just as the market was opening up for the day. As they wove through the busy crowd, Benvolio's shoulder brushed against another.

He looked up to see Tybalt, nephew of Lord and Lady Capulet, glaring at him. Benvolio jumped back – Tybalt was the last person he wanted to see.

"Benvolio Montague," Tybalt growled, drawing his sword. "I'll kill you!"

"Peace," Benvolio begged, holding up his hands. "I only want to keep the peace."

"Peace?" Tybalt seethed. "I hate the word, as I hate all Montagues and YOU!" With his eyes wide and his nostrils flared, he lunged at Benvolio.

Without a second thought, Mercutio drew his sword and flew to help his friend. Steel clashed on steel, and chaos descended upon the square.

As if from nowhere, Lord Montague leaped through the crowd, leading a gang of angry men. "Down with the Capulets!" they cried.

Seconds later, Lord Capulet appeared with a group of Capulets behind him. "Down with the

Montagues!" they roared. Screams and insults flew, and the two warring families fell upon each other.

In the midst of the fighting, a loud voice bellowed across the square.

"Enough!" Everybody froze: it was Prince Escalus, the ruler of Verona.

"Throw your weapons to the ground!" Prince Escalus roared, striding into the middle of all the commotion. There was a clatter of metal as all Montagues and Capulets dropped their swords.

Prince Escalus scowled. "If you ever disturb the peace in our streets again," he said furiously, "you will pay the price with your lives!"

As the sun set across Verona, everybody at the Capulet house was busy preparing for a masked ball. Juliet Capulet was excited – she was young, and it was the first ball that her parents, Lord and Lady Capulet, had allowed her to attend.

As she spun around her bedroom in a dazzling embroidered gold gown, she took her nurse's hand. "Dance with me, Nurse!" she laughed.

The nurse chuckled and rolled her eyes. "Ah, Juliet, you're such a pretty child," she said. She'd looked after Juliet since she was a baby, and was deeply fond of the girl. "I can't believe you're so grown up now."

Just then, the bedroom door swung open, and Lord and Lady Capulet swept in.

"Juliet, darling," Lady Capulet said. "We have some important news to tell you." She looked Juliet up and down, and gave a small nod of approval. "You're soon to be married."

Juliet gasped. "Married?"

Lady Capulet glanced at her husband. "Yes, Juliet. It's about time. Why, I was already married to your father at your age."

Lord Capulet sniffed. "We've found a suitable match for you, Juliet, and you shall be introduced to him tonight, at the ball."

Juliet's cheeks flushed red. "Who is he?"

"Count Paris," Lady Capulet replied, clasping her daughter's hand. "My dear, you can't want for anything more. He's handsome and wealthy – and he's asked for you to be his wife!" Her eyes glistened. "What do you say?"

Suddenly, Juliet felt lightheaded. She sat down on the edge of her bed. "I-I suppose I'll meet him," she said, carefully. She glanced at her mother and father, who were waiting expectantly. "And I hope to like him when I do."

Candles twinkled all around the grand hall, and the sound of music filled the air. Costumed men in glittering masks whirled women across the dance floor – a sea of rustling silk dresses and heavy brocade. The Capulet ball had begun.

Romeo, hoping to catch a glimpse of Rosaline, pulled a mask across his eyes and slipped into the back of the hall. Mercutio and Benvolio, similarly masked, followed close behind him.

"Don't let your masks slip, boys," Mercutio hissed. "If anyone spots a Montague here, we're in big trouble."

Romeo nodded and edged onto the dance floor, scanning the guests for Rosaline. Instead, his eyes fell upon a beautiful young girl, dressed in an embroidered gold gown. She was dancing with another man, gliding across the dance floor, looking as graceful as a dove. In that very moment, Romeo completely forgot about Rosaline.

"Who's *she*?" he whispered, nudging Mercutio. "I swear I've never seen true beauty until tonight."

"Her name is Juliet Capulet," Mercutio whispered back. He glanced at Romeo. "She's the daughter of your greatest enemy!"

Romeo didn't flinch. His eyes were still fixed on Juliet. He watched as she moved across the dance floor, bewitched by her intelligent green eyes and dimpled smile.

He didn't care that she was a Capulet – he just had to dance with her at once.

"Let's go," Mercutio urged, as the dance ended and the music stopped. "Come on, Romeo."

But Romeo ignored him, and slipped through the crowd towards Juliet. Bending down on one knee, he took Juliet's hand gently. "May I have this dance?" he whispered.

Surprised, Juliet laughed. "Of course."

Romeo stood up and swept Juliet into the middle of the dance floor. Then they began to dance. As they whirled across the floor, they moved with such style and grace, the other guests stepped back to watch.

"Who is the masked stranger?" Whispers rippled through the crowd.

Count Paris scowled. "Who is that man dancing with my future wife?"

But neither Romeo nor Juliet heard a sound; they were entirely lost in the dance.

Juliet stared into the masked stranger's deep brown eyes. "Who are you?" she whispered.

Romeo was about to open his mouth to speak, when his mask slipped from his face and onto the

floor. Panicked, he let go of Juliet's arms.

"ROMEO MONTAGUE!" a voice roared. "I'll kill you!" It was Tybalt Capulet, barging onto the dance floor with his fists clenched.

Juliet gasped. "A Montague?"

Tybalt seized Romeo and pinned him up against a pillar. "Villain!" he growled, his eyes flashing with anger. "What are you doing here?"

Before Romeo could reply, someone grabbed Tybalt roughly from behind. It was Lord Capulet.

"Come now, gentlemen," Lord Capulet said sternly, pulling his nephew back. "There'll be no fighting inside this house!"

Tybalt reluctantly let go. "As you wish, uncle," he muttered, before skulking away.

Romeo let out a sigh of relief. "Thank you, Lord Capulet," he said.

"Ignore him," Lord Capulet said. "I'd rather not upset Prince Escalus again... so you may join our guests if you wish." He smiled begrudgingly, then disappeared off into the crowd.

It was the early hours of the morning, and all was quiet in the Capulet house. The guests had departed and everybody was fast asleep.

Everybody except Juliet.

"Oh Romeo, Romeo! Why do you have to be a Montague?" Juliet leaned over her bedroom balcony and stared into the moonlit sky. She hadn't even had a chance to say goodbye to Romeo – her mother had whisked her away at the first hint of a fight. She longed to see him again.

Looking down at the garden below, she noticed a figure darting through the shadows. Moments later, Romeo emerged from the undergrowth, just beneath her window.

Juliet gasped. "How did you get here?"

Romeo gazed up at her earnestly. "I climbed the garden walls to see you."

Juliet glanced over her shoulder nervously. "If any of my family sees you here, you'll be in great danger!"

"I don't care," Romeo whispered defiantly.

"Oh Juliet, please tell me you love me, as I love you!" He extended his arm up to her.

Juliet paused for a moment, then carefully climbed down some small steps into the garden below. "I love you," she said softly, as he swept her up in his arms.

Under the light of the moon, the young lovers began to dance once more. Spinning across the soft, dewy grass, they twirled between rose beds and leaped over low hedges.

"I'm afraid this is too sweet to be real," Romeo whispered breathlessly, as they finished the dance.

Juliet bit her lip. "If you truly love me, and you want to marry me," she said, "I will send my nurse to you tomorrow." She gazed at him intently. "Tell her where and what time we shall be wed."

Romeo nodded. "I will," he replied. "Send her to the town square at nine o'clock tomorrow

morning. I'll be waiting for her there."

"I love you," whispered Juliet again, her heart pounding in her chest. "But now I must be gone. Good night, good night!" She smiled ruefully, before slipping away into the house.

The next morning, a crowd of chattering townspeople gathered in the town square. It was festival season in the city of Verona, and lively jesters were performing tricks, while acrobats somersaulted through the air.

In a corner of the square, Romeo sat on a step, staring into space. He couldn't stop thinking about last night – had it really happened?

Just then, a silvery-haired woman came marching towards him. "Romeo?" she asked.

Romeo's heart leapt, and he jumped up eagerly.

"Yes, that's me. Are you Juliet's nurse?"

The nurse nodded. "I have a letter here from Juliet for you."

Romeo reached out to take it, but the nurse snatched it away. "Can I trust you?" she scowled. "My lady Juliet is young. Will you be true to her?"

"Yes, trust me, for I adore her," Romeo assured the nurse. "Please tell her I have arranged for us to be married this afternoon, at Friar Lawrence's chapel. She'll have to sneak out of her house without her parents noticing."

A broad smile spread across the nurse's face and she gave Romeo a big hug. "Heaven bless you!"

"Give my compliments to Juliet," Romeo laughed, gently untangling himself from her arms.

"Yes, a thousand times." She handed Romeo Juliet's letter, and hurried off through the crowd.

That afternoon, Romeo and Juliet met at Friar

Lawrence's chapel to be married.

"I hope this union will end the conflict between your two families," Friar Lawrence said, as he finished his blessing.

Romeo squeezed Juliet's hand. "I'm so happy," he whispered.

"I love you more than words can say," Juliet replied, kissing him tenderly. "Now I'd better get home, before anyone notices I'm gone."

The newlyweds thanked Friar Lawrence for his kindness, and left the chapel.

Back in the town square, Romeo found the festivities in full swing. He spotted his friends, Mercutio and Benvolio, sitting by a water fountain, and wandered over to greet them.

"Romeo!" Mercutio smiled, giving him a playful punch. "Where have you been all afternoon?"

Romeo shrugged. "Oh, nowhere," he lied.

Spotting Tybalt walking towards them, Mercutio lowered his voice. "Uh-oh, watch out friends. Here comes trouble."

"Romeo, you villain!" Tybalt cursed. He'd not forgotten about Romeo's unwelcome appearance at the masked ball.

As Romeo backed away, his mind started to whir. Tybalt was Juliet's cousin – her own flesh and blood. Romeo was now part of Juliet's family. "I am no villain," he said softly. "In fact, your name, Capulet, is as dear to me as my own!"

"Liar," hissed Tybalt, drawing his sword.

"Who are you calling a liar?" Mercutio yelled, pulling out his dagger.

"Please don't!" cried Romeo, trying to step between them.

But no one listened. The clash of weapons echoed fatally in the cobbled square. Death was swift and ruthless. In a moment, Mercutio lay still, and Tybalt's sword dripped with blood.

Seeing his friend lying dead on the ground, all reason deserted Romeo. Red-hot anger flooded his mind, and he leaped forward and plunged his own sword into Tybalt's heart. Tybalt slumped to the ground, and Romeo stood over him, aghast.

"Oh, I am fortune's fool!" Romeo cried in a fit of emotion, before staggering away from the scene.

The noise of the scuffle brought people rushing over, including Prince Escalus and Juliet's parents, Lord and Lady Capulet.

Lady Capulet collapsed on the ground next to Tybalt. "Oh my nephew!" she groaned.

Prince Escalus looked at the two murdered men, their short lives wasted. "Benvolio," he said, sharply. "Who began this bloody fight?"

"T-T-Tybalt began it... T-T-Tybalt killed

Mercutio," Benvolio stuttered. "Romeo didn't want to fight at all. He was trying to stop them…"

"Romeo killed Tybalt?" Lady Capulet snapped, looking up. "Then Romeo must die!"

Prince Escalus glanced sympathetically at Lady Capulet. "For this crime," he said, raising his voice so everybody could hear, "Romeo is exiled. Never shall he show his face here in Verona again, on pain of death."

Juliet woke with a start. "Romeo?" She rubbed her eyes as daylight flooded in through her window.

"I must be gone," Romeo whispered, already up. He bent down to kiss her cheek.

Juliet yawned and sat up in bed. "Please, stay a while," she begged, desperate not to be parted from her husband. "I don't know when I'll see you again."

"I'm afraid I must leave," Romeo replied. "You know what the prince said. If I stay in Verona much longer, I will die."

Juliet kissed him, her heart ready to burst with sorrow. "Farewell, my love," she whispered.

Reluctantly, Romeo crept across her bedroom and disappeared over the balcony.

Juliet sighed and climbed out of bed. Just then, her nurse rushed in.

"Your parents are on their way," the nurse said, anxiously. "And they're bringing Count Paris – the man you're *supposed* to be engaged to!"

Juliet turned pale. "What am I going to do?" Her voice was full of panic. With shaking hands, she tied up her dress and smoothed her hair.

The nurse clucked her tongue, but before she could think what to say, the door swung open and Lady Capulet walked in.

"I bring joyful news, child!" Lady Capulet announced cheerfully. "Your father and Count Paris are here to discuss the details of your wedding on Thursday."

Juliet let out a low moan and buried her face in the nurse's apron. "I won't marry him!" she said, through her sobs.

Lady Capulet frowned. "That's enough, Juliet." she said, her voice suddenly cold.

"What are these tears, Juliet?" Lord Capulet asked, as he breezed into the room with Count Paris. "Dry your eyes, child, for Count Paris is here to speak with you!"

Juliet sniffed and stared at the floor.

"How delighted I am to see you, my lady," said Count Paris, walking over to plant a kiss on Juliet's cheek. "Are you all ready for our wedding?"

Juliet whimpered, and a tear rolled down her cheek. "I can't marry you," she said, softly. "I'm sorry, but I don't love you."

There was a brief, awkward silence. Count Paris turned to Lord Capulet for help.

"Pardon?" Lord Capulet thundered, his face crumpling up with rage. "What did you say, girl?"

"I'm sorry, Father," Juliet whispered. "But if you'll just listen to me..."

Lord Capulet lifted up a finger to silence her. "If you do not marry Count Paris on Thursday," he bellowed, "I shall no longer call you my daughter."

Juliet's lips moved as if to speak, but she didn't make a sound.

"Ungrateful child," Lord Capulet said. "Come, Count Paris. Leave her." He stormed out of the bedroom, with Lady Capulet and Count Paris following close behind.

"Oh Nurse," Juliet said, her whole body shaking. "What on earth am I to do?"

"I don't know, child," the nurse replied, closing the door gently. "I just don't know."

Friar Lawrence was quietly reading in his chapel, when Juliet burst in.

"Help me, Friar!" she cried, desperately. She sank to her knees. "My parents are trying to force me to marry Count Paris! What shall I do?"

Friar Lawrence looked up from his book with deep concern. "Now, child," he said, slowly rising from his chair. "Do not despair."

He began to pace back and forth. After some time, he spoke. "There is something you can do," he began hesitantly.

"Go on, Father," Juliet said, sensing a glimmer of hope in his voice.

"Go home, Juliet, and agree to marry Count Paris," Friar Lawrence said. "But take this with you…" He took a key from his pocket and unlocked a small cupboard in the corner of the chapel. From it, he took out a tiny bottle of liquid. "Drink this potion before you go to bed, and you will fall into a deathlike sleep," he said, pressing the bottle into Juliet's hand. "Your body will turn cold and everyone will believe you are dead. Your parents will take you to the family vault, where you'll be laid out on a marble tombstone."

Juliet inspected the bottle in her hand, piecing together the Friar's desperate plan.

"After forty-two hours, you shall awake," the Friar continued. "You'll feel as if you've just had a long, deep sleep. Meanwhile, I will send Romeo a message to come and rescue you, so you and he can run away together."

Juliet nodded. "Thank you, Father," she said. Then she gritted her teeth. "Love give me strength." She slipped the bottle into her pocket, and disappeared out through the chapel door.

Back at the Capulet house, Juliet found her parents in the sitting room.

"Where have you been?" Lord Capulet snapped.

"To speak with Friar Lawrence," Juliet replied.

"He told me to ask for your forgiveness, and accept Count Paris's hand in marriage."

A flicker of a smile passed over Lord Capulet's face. "And...?"

"I'm sorry, Father," Juliet said quietly. "I take back what I said – I agree to marry Count Paris."

Pleased, Lord Capulet nodded curtly.

"Now I'd like to go to bed," Juliet continued, pretending to stifle a yawn. "It will be a long day tomorrow, with all the festivities."

Kissing both her father and mother on the cheek, Juliet walked out of the sitting room and climbed up the stairs to her bedroom. Once inside, she shut the door and sank down onto her bed.

"Romeo, Romeo, Romeo!" she whispered, clutching the potion bottle. "I drink to you!"

Then she put the bottle to her lips and emptied its contents down her throat.

Two days later, a crowd of mourners gathered together to pay their respects as Juliet's casket was carried down into the family vault.

"Wretched, hateful day!" Lady Capulet sobbed.

"Oh woeful, woeful day!" the nurse wept.

None of Juliet's family could believe what had happened – Juliet had been found cold and pale in her bed the day before, with an empty bottle of what looked like poison by her side.

As evening fell and everybody went home, the vault fell deathly quiet. Then, in the gloom, a chink of light fell upon Juliet's casket. Romeo was walking down the stone steps into the vault.

"Oh my love, my wife!" he cried out, on seeing Juliet lying still in the dark. "Death has sucked all the honey from your breath."

He let out an agonizing wail, which echoed

around the cavern. For Romeo had never received Friar Lawrence's message.

Instead, after fleeing Verona, he had heard the news of Juliet's death from a stranger – and had returned to the city immediately. Friar Lawrence *had* written to tell him that Juliet was not really dead, but the letter had arrived too late.

Now, all Romeo had with him was a vial of poison, with which he planned to kill himself. He gazed down at Juliet's body. She looked as though she was only asleep, but when he reached out to touch her hand, it was icy cold.

"Eyes take your last look," he said to himself. Then he put the vial of poison to his lips and drank every last drop. "So with a kiss, I die," he breathed, kissing Juliet one last time.

Within seconds, the poison flooded Romeo's

veins. His body quickly turned cold, and he collapsed dead on the steps beneath Juliet's casket.

For a short while, everything was quiet. Then, Juliet stirred. Gradually, the bloom returned to her cheeks and her eyes fluttered open. She was finally awake.

Juliet stood up slowly from her marble tombstone. Peering around the vault, her eyes fell upon a body lying on the floor. It took her a few moments to recognize it as the body of her husband, Romeo.

"Romeo, is that you?" she whispered. Still unsteady on her feet, she stumbled over to him. "Romeo!" she cried, shaking him. There was no response. Then she noticed a vial in his open hand… "What's this?" she whimpered. "Poison?" Slowly, it dawned upon her that her husband was dead – that he must have poisoned himself, not realizing that she still lived. "You drank it all, and left no drop to help me?" She flung the empty bottle to the ground.

Juliet's decision was quick. She pulled out the dagger attached to Romeo's belt.

"Let me die," she whispered. Then she plunged the dagger deep into her side. Her body fell over his, and the rose of her blood bloomed over them both.

Night fell and a grieving Count Paris arrived at the Capulet vault. As he walked down the steps, he stopped short and let out a terrible scream. To his horror, he could see it contained *two* bodies...

Romeo and Juliet were lying together on the stone floor. White lilies from Juliet's casket were scattered all around.

Before long, the gloomy vault was full of people:

Romeo's parents, Juliet's parents, her nurse, Prince Escalus and Friar Lawrence. Nobody could understand what had happened until finally, Friar Lawrence broke the silence. As he explained how the deaths must have happened, he begged forgiveness for his part in the tragedy.

"Oh, brother Montague," Lord Capulet sobbed, reaching out to Lord Montague with a shaking hand. "Give me your hand."

"Willingly," Lord Montague replied, breaking down in bitter tears.

After decades of fighting, the old enemies clasped each other, drawn together by their grief.

Prince Escalus looked on, his expression full of sorrow as he murmured, "There never was a story of more woe, than that of Juliet and her Romeo."

Usborne Quicklinks

For links to websites where you can watch video clips of dancers performing in the ballets retold in this book and find out more about the stories, characters and music, go to the Usborne Quicklinks website at **www.usborne.com/quicklinks** and enter the keywords "ballet stories". Please follow the online safety guidelines at the Usborne Quicklinks website.

Designed by Lenka Hrehova & Tabitha Blore
Digital manipulation: Nick Wakeford
Edited by Rosie Dickins & Lesley Sims

First published in 2018 by Usborne Publishing Ltd., 83-85 Saffron Hill, London EC1N 8RT, England. www.usborne.com Copyright © 2018 Usborne Publishing Limited. The name Usborne and the devices ♀⊕ are Trade Marks of Usborne Publishing Ltd.
First published in America in 2018. UE.